Crack the Spine
Winter 2013

Edited by Kerri Farrell Foley

ISBN-13: **978-0988978201**
ISBN-10: **0988978202**

CONTENTS

The Oxford Hotel

In December 2001

they're giving it away

in lower Denver, the swirly

walk of Wazee, black

mornings when the half-lived

sleep and grope up 17th.

Slow trains crawl only

during pre-dawn. 23

nights for me at the Oxford

in one glass-frosted year.

I have wanted you here.

This slick lobby glows

but upstairs, my dear, you see

the armoires groan and open,

petulant, drawers stay

and flop, and showers lead

their own separate lives.

It's being given away now.

No one will travel, climb

black four-posters; no one

needs a dark ride out.

Small-town boy, I want

one night to steal your drinks,

dance in your dreams, unfold

your coat. This is not

about buckling, this is

solely about fear, a way

of thinking and running,

avoiding the rockslides.

You can't fly there forever.

The time is now. I lost

the quick ironic posture

that once tucked me in safely

under matelasse, lamplight, down
and alone. So lovesick I didn't
breathe. Now I cannot leave.

Remember? The doomed tangling
of the truly damaged.
Watch me lose sight, grasp

the scald of lost mornings.
Tear your own admission
ticket. Wynkoop reeks

and forgets in moonlight.
I thought you might
need me to break your fall,

but only cold trains reach out
Denver nights, so you cracked
my fake heart. Everything's

free now. I will not return
to the Oxford Hotel. I'm counting
the rate on my fingers, in dimes.

Food for the Gods

Charlotte couldn't see the roses through the mass of dead and dying bamboo outside her bedroom window. Edward had promised to cut the stuff down and dig up the roots, but Edward had also promised to save money for their retirement so they could travel the world. Now Edward was dead and there was no money. Charlotte wasn't going anywhere – except, today, to see a realtor about selling the house -- and the bamboo had taken over the yard. Marcy, her daughter, had told her that some people were interested in growing bamboo, that Charlotte should advertise it in the paper. "And don't forget, Mother," she'd lectured in the squeaky, school-teacherish voice that grated so on Charlotte's nerves, "some people eat bamboo shoots as a delicacy. You should try them."

That would be the day.

Charlotte got out of bed and stooped to make it, groaning as the arthritis pinched at her fingers and took a bite out of her shoulder. She worked until each corner was perfect and not a wrinkle marred the spread. The house would show well. It was spotless and, since she'd gotten rid of everything that had belonged to Edward, uncluttered. It pleased her that she had made a little over six hundred dollars by selling his things at a yard sale. He'd been such a collector: humidors and pipes, miniature metal soldiers, old-fashioned fountain pens, bamboo.

He'd told her once that bamboo flowered everywhere in the world at the exact same time. "Imagine that, Lottie," he'd said, his arm outstretched as if to encompass the globe, a pipe curled in his fingers, sending waves of Cherry Blend tobacco into the room, "each and every plant – millions, probably – in China and India, Africa and South

America and right here in Oregon – flowering at the same moment. It's a miracle!"

A miracle. A miracle would have been if he'd kept his word and left her something besides his memory and the grand plans he'd had for them. That would have been the miracle.

Charlotte still couldn't figure out what he'd done with the money. Yes, the Meerschaum pipes had cost a lot, and antique pens didn't come cheap, but after all those years of working and saving – at least he'd said he'd been saving – where had it gone? She was starting to think that there was another woman somewhere, standing furred and jeweled at the window of a penthouse, wondering whatever had happened to her sugar daddy.

At nine, Charlotte locked the front door and walked three blocks to New Age Realty, hoping the name referred to the new millennium rather than to some superstitious attitude of the salespeople who worked there. A grim smile passed across her face as she imagined a woman swathed in fringed silk scarves lighting candles and incense in every room of her little bungalow, protecting it against curtain pullers and thieves.

The sound of what looked to be Nepalese bells attached to New Age's heavy glass doors reminded her of Marcy's voice and made her wince. But, then a woman came toward her, a sensible looking, conventionally dressed, middle-aged woman with a friendly smile, and Charlotte relaxed.

"Good morning! I'm Sally Fairweather. You must be Mrs. Blackborn?"

"Charlotte, please."

"Welcome, Charlotte. Come sit down and tell me about your house."

Half an hour later, they were pulling up to Charlotte's bungalow in Sally's shiny late model gold Cadillac. It was just the sort of comfortable, quiet car Edward had talked about buying after he retired so they could travel the country in luxury. Getting to New Orleans and Savannah, Chicago and New York, would have been effortless in a car like Sally Fairweather's. Charlotte inhaled the new leather smell and decided not to feel bad about it.

When they pulled up in front of the house, Sally said, "Oh! Cute!" She turned off the engine and pushed open the Caddy's thick door with her booted foot. "It's got great street appeal, Charlotte."

Charlotte was trying to see her home through the eyes of a stranger and decided that it was, indeed, a charming little house. Two strips of bright grass held the sidewalk tightly between them, and picked up the green of geranium-laden flower boxes beneath the windows on either side of the white-painted front door. Lace curtains gave it an old-fashioned feel, and the polished brass doorknocker, shaped like an elephant's head, provided a touch of whimsy. Charlotte thought that if she were in the market for a house, this one would be at the top of her list.

"What's in the back yard? The fringed stuff that's poking up over the roof?" Sally asked, turning her face up into the sun.

"Bamboo. My husband was a great fan of it."

Sally grimaced. "Bamboo? My goodness, it's so tall! And so untidy looking."

Charlotte was fumbling with her front door key, angry all over again with Edward. Stupid, stupid, stupid Edward, messing up her life from the grave. She tried a smile in Sally's direction. "The inside is lovely. Please, come in." She pushed opened the door and Sally began grinning again.

"Oh!" she said, "It's adorable!"

Charlotte breathed easy as she watched Sally's eyes scan the living room. Instead of Edward's books and magazines cluttering the end tables, the polished bare wood gleamed. Lace had replaced the heavy, damask curtains, and the sunlight cast floral patterns on the bright white walls. Charlotte had taken down Edward's painting of the Spanish Armada on rough Channel seas and replaced it with an inexpensive, but lovely, pastel of a woman in a bustle walking along a sunny beach, carrying a parasol. All the room needed was a crystal vase of her beautiful roses, and it would be perfect.

"This is wonderful," Sally said, giving Charlotte an admiring look. "You have the knack."

It had been so long since she'd had a compliment that, instead of crying, Charlotte merely bit her lip and led Sally into the single bath and then into two small bedrooms.

"This room doesn't fit with the others," Sally said, eyeing the bedroom that Charlotte and Edward had shared for forty-four years. "It's so dark."

"I know. The bamboo."

"I can see that. My goodness, there's so much of it!"

Charlotte nodded. "We might as well go into the back yard."

The two women walked through the short hall and into the kitchen, as bright as Charlotte could make it with the bamboo preventing any but the sharpest rays of sun from making it to the window. She heard Sally mutter 'too bad,' and then they were outside on the tiny patio, surrounded by bamboo, a fringe of green now and then breaking the monotony of tall, thin stalks of pale brown.

Charlotte stood still. "The Japanese believed that their gods could be found in the stems of the bamboo plant," she said. "My husband once told me that bamboo has been a symbol of good fortune in Asian cultures for more than four thousand years."

Sally gave her an odd look, but Charlotte couldn't stop.

"He also said that the very first chopsticks were made of bamboo. The Japanese people used then whenever they offered food to the gods."

Sally said nothing, just crossed her arms in front of her chest and stared at the dense mess that was now Charlotte's back yard. Charlotte pulled at her thumbnail and took a deep breath. "I can't afford to have it removed. He didn't leave me anything but the house and his social security. He ran his own business and there was no pension."

Sally nodded and pursed her lips. "Well. This is a problem," she said. "Didn't you mention a child?"

"My daughter. But she's –" Charlotte waved her hand in the air – "flighty. Marcy would be no help at all." Charlotte backed up until she felt the edge of the seat of an old lawn chair graze her skirt and sat down, feeling the weight of a thousand stalks of bamboo on her shoulders. If she didn't sell the house, the rest of her life would be hopeless.

Nearing panic, she asked the realtor, "Do you suppose anyone would want it? The bamboo, I mean. Cuttings, perhaps? There must be some way of getting rid of it."

Sally turned to face her. "If everything was in good shape, your property would be worth about two hundred thousand dollars. I suppose someone will buy it with this – mess – back here, but you won't get top dollar." She scanned Charlotte's slumping figure with a critical eye. "Are you strong enough to do it yourself?"

Charlotte felt bitter. "I'm sixty-five, I'm not dead yet." Embarrassed, she shook her head and looked into Sally's eyes. "I'm sorry. It's arthritis. My back and shoulders hurt nearly all the time. I wanted to see my roses again after Edward died, so I tried cutting the bamboo back and it was very painful." She straightened her spine and leaned away from the back of the lawn chair. "I can try again."

Sally nodded. "Well, why don't you give it a shot. Or borrow some money against the house. You said it's nearly paid off? Your bank would probably give you a home equity loan." She looked at her watch. "I'll come back next week and see how it's going. If you could just get a path to the wall – I presume that's where the roses are? -- it would make a big difference to a prospective buyer to at least be able to see to the end of the property." She pulled her keys from her purse and gave Charlotte a tight smile. "I'll let myself out."

When she heard the front door slam, Charlotte forced herself up out of the chair and went back into the kitchen, noticing once again how dim the room was. She poured herself a glass of water from the carafe in the refrigerator and picked up the phone. Maybe Marcy could help.

"Oh, Mother, you can't do that! You'll hurt yourself! I'll come over on Saturday after my art class and work on it for – Oh! No, I can't on Saturday. That's the day the Garden Club is having it's – and Sunday? Sunday I've got church and then there's a luncheon, and our book discussion group afterward. Karl would never miss that! But I'll come by after work one day next week, I promise. If I can. Okay?"

"Of course, dear. And thank you." Charlotte put the phone down and rubbed her shoulder again. "Damn you, Edward," she said. He'd spoiled the child since the day of her birth, indulging her every whim, treating her like royalty. Fortunately, Marcy had married a rich man, though not a generous one. No, Karl wasn't the sort of man to go begging money from, even if it was just a loan to pay some gardeners with. She'd just have to do it herself, and that was that.

It was cloudy when she awoke the next morning. Clouds made her back hurt, but it would make working outdoors easier. Clouds would cover the sun and sunlight wasn't good for a woman with a propensity for migraine. Charlotte dressed and fixed herself toast and tea for breakfast before finding the gloves and hat she had once worn while tending the roses.

The roses. She'd planted American Heritage first, falling in love with the creamy yellow color the first time she'd seen them at a gardening show. She'd bought a plant and watched it grow, delighted when the first blossoms held a tinge of pink so barely there that it almost seemed like fairy dust. Then Edward had surprised her with her namesake rose, the deep pink Charlotte Armstrong that turned pale red when it bloomed. He'd also given her a rose-red Rubaiyat for their forty-third wedding anniversary. And then he'd brought home the blasted bamboo and, before she knew it, the path to the roses was been cut off. They'd gotten water -- Edward always watered -- but they hadn't been fed in a couple of years. Even though she knew they wouldn't thrive without rose food, she was pretty sure they still lived.

She found a saw in the storage room off the patio, then decided to use pruning shears to cut the stalks down first and dig up the roots later. It would be tough going; she'd be on her hands and knees for the root part, since they were on the surface but also down below. Everywhere she'd dig she'd hit roots, which she'd then have to pry out of the ground. She took the implements onto the patio and looked down and away from the forest of stalks, just in case she might lose her courage.

For two hours she lopped at the bamboo, pretending she was a warrior cutting down the enemy, taking a ten minute break in order to drag the trash can to the front gate. The city only picked up garbage twice a week – on Mondays and Thursdays. Today was Friday, so there'd be quite a pile of bamboo for the next pick-up, but she didn't think she could afford to have someone other than the city garbage men haul it away.

It was hard work, and by eleven, when she stopped for a drink of water, she was dismayed to see that she'd accomplished very little, although the trash can was filled with stalks and leaves and the wispy flowers that reminded her of paint brushes. She had bent the tall poles in half, then broken them into smaller pieces, and her hands, as well as her back and neck, were sore. She felt dizzy, too, and more breathless than she liked. The water was refreshing, but when the glass was empty, she saw it begin to fill up again with tears.

On the second day, she cleared a narrow path about six feet long and the width of her shoulders. She could barely squeeze through it, slight as she was, but looking at the emptiness gave her a tiny bit of hope. She had bundled up the stalks that wouldn't fit into the trash can and laid them on the patio with the intent of refilling the can as soon as it was emptied Monday.

That night, Sally called her. "How's it going?"

"It's coming along. I won't be finished in a week, though."

"Well, that's okay. I'll figure on an open house in two weeks. Have you hired anybody?"

"No. I've made up my mind to do it myself."

Sally was quiet. "Whatever you decide, Charlotte. But, remember, the better the place looks, the more money you'll get."

"I know."

"Okay. I'll talk to you next week. Take care."

Charlotte put the receiver back in its rack and turned up the radio, listening for the weather report. So far the clouds were cooperating with her plans, but the forecasters had bright sunshine in sight for the middle of the week. It was hard going with the arthritis, but a migraine would put her to bed for days.

She awoke to the sound of her neighbors leaving on vacation. It was still dark, but the extra expenditure of energy over the last couple of days had made her hungry. She sipped juice and ate a toasted muffin as she watched the sun come up, barely visible beneath the dense cloud cover. With relief, she went to the back, this time starting on her knees, grateful that she'd found her old kneepads in the storage room.

The first dizzy spell hit her about an hour into her work. The dizziness was coming more frequently and it worried her, especially since she hadn't been to the doctor since Edward's death six months before. Her heart wasn't strong. She wished she could pray for health and safety – and money enough to live out her years without having to beg from Karl and Marcy -- but the belief in a higher power had disappeared along with Edward. She had no choice but to persist in her endeavor and hope she'd be able to sell the house, rent a small apartment, and invest the remainder wisely. Perhaps she could get a job selling dresses or kitchen implements at one of the department stores downtown.

The thoughts tramping throughout her brain all ended in the same place: Why had she ever let Edward talk her into staying home and taking care of him? She didn't know who she was maddest at: Edward for suggesting it, or herself for falling into his plans so easily, so trustingly.

At ten, she got up and went for water. Standing on the patio, she looked down the narrow aisle she'd sweated over and shook her head in amazement at the power of the plant. All that work – days of it – and she'd barely made a dent.

Back on her knees, she removed her glove to get better purchase of a small vein of root. She tugged and pulled at it, making her shoulder burn, until it came out with a pop and landed her on her rump. She saw a glint of metal beneath it and knelt again, wiggling the smaller roots back and forth until she could see it clearly. An hour later, her neck so sore that tears lay on her lashes, she had cleared away the dirt and roots from what looked to be square piece of metal. Try as she might, she couldn't get it out of the ground. "After lunch," she told herself.

As she was eating her sandwich, Charlotte ran the answering machine. Marcy had called. "Just checking in, Mother. I wanted you to know that Karl needs me to run some errands for him, so I won't be able to come by and help you any earlier than next Thursday. You take care, now, Mother and don't work too hard." Charlotte hung up and put the rest of the sandwich on the plate. The sun was coming out; not a good thing. She decided to finish lunch later.

She took a small spade from the storage room and began to work it down the sides of what was turning out to be a metal box. By 2 p.m. she had exposed about an inch in all directions, but she still couldn't budge it, and the clasp – a long one – was still buried. She couldn't tell yet if it needed a key, but who would bury a metal box without a lock?

As the sun came out from behind the clouds, shining its full face upon her, the answer came to her: Edward. Edward! Had he saved after all? Had all the ugly feelings she'd had about him for the past six months been for nothing?

Frantic now, she scraped and jiggled, while the dull heaviness of an impending migraine sat waiting at the base of her skull. "Please god, please god, please god," she muttered, sweat staining the ground around her. The migraine slammed her just as she exposed the clasp. In agony, her eyes alight with the aura from the headache, she opened the box. Stacks of bills – she couldn't know yet how deep they went – bundled with rubber bands met her fingers. She stuffed some of them in her blouse, in the pockets of her pants, and tried to stand. Her knees gave out and she crumpled on the ground, scraping her cheek on the sharp and dirty edge of the box lid. She could feel wetness, but she didn't care. Money. She had money. Edward had been telling her the truth after all.

She struggled to rise, and this time her knees held. Stooped, with the packs of money rubbing against the skin beneath her clothes, she made her way to the patio. She would wait out the headache and then she'd count it. There would be thousands, she was sure. Enough to keep her from having to sell the house. Maybe enough to be able to travel.

The headache was a killer. She needed the drugs that would make her sleep. Still blinded by the aura, she bumped, hard, into the door frame, felt moisture, realigned herself and made it into the kitchen. Fumbling for the bottle in the cabinet with one hand, she picked up her water glass with the other. One pill, two; she'd feel the effects soon.

Not caring that she was filthy with dirt and sweat, she made her way into the bedroom and lay down on top of the spread, pulling the piles of money from inside her clothes, holding them to her chest, wishing she could see the bills, find out just how much she had.

She slept, and dreamed. She was on a cruise ship, standing at the railing, looking out at a tropical island. The wind blew her hair – blonde and long, again – and she was inhaling deeply, smelling the salt of the sea. On the distant shore, palms were bending gracefully to the music of steel drums, and, content, she leaned backwards into the arms of her lover. She couldn't see him, but his hands, which held her elbows, were strong and tan. He nuzzled her neck and whispered into her ear. In her sleep, she smiled. "I'll always take care of you," he was saying, and she turned to look at him. It was Edward, young and handsome, virile and strong, his dark eyes penetrating. "Always."

When she awoke, the headache was better and she was hungry. When she sat up, the money fell off her body onto the bedspread. She had collected twelve packets, bound by rubber bands, some rotting. One had broken, and bills were strewn on the sheets; they'd slid onto the floor. Twenties. They were all twenties. Edward had thought he'd take care of her with twenties.

Fifty twenties to a bundle, maybe forty bundles. She tried to do the math in her head, but it hurt too much. She reached into the drawer of her bedside table and got paper and pencil. Forty thousand dollars. Ten thousand for each year they'd been together. Hardly anything, really.

Disappointed, she lay back down and sighed, fingering the money. Forty thousand. At least she could afford to pay to have the bamboo cut down. Then she'd get top dollar for the house and go back home to Missouri. It would be cheaper to live there and she thought there might be a cousin or two left. She'd invest the money, get an apartment, plant roses – an Eiffel Tower first, then an Arizona and an Oklahoma – pink, orange, dark red. She'd tend her roses, grow old, and die alone. Marcy and Karl would be relieved to be rid of her.

It was a plan. Not what she'd hoped for, but then a thought wiggled its way through the headache. Had Edward buried more? Could there be another metal box beneath the roots of the bamboo? Or, better yet, two or three? Far-fetched, but possible.

She was only 65, not 85, she thought, which meant there was plenty of time to travel. Pushing away thoughts of cruise ships and palm trees, she reached for the phone and left a message: "Sally, this is Charlotte. Thank you for your help with the house, but I've decided to take it off the market." By the time she hung up, the headache was gone.

One Life to Live

It could be treason or a white-haired angel

perched atop the dewdrop magnifying

a swallowtail's iodine mascara.

It could be that.

Then again, it could be treason

or a politician dressed as treason;

hard to tell.

Or it could be nothing at all,

just a repositioning of plates,

tectonic or cerebellum.

It could be the separation

of marrow from bone, how unfortunate,

but as soon as one speculates,

one has the suspicion that one

wouldn't know one if one saw one.

So, rain-soaked, red accordion ribs

switching thumbs in a crow infested,

stubble field, Vincent slouched

his canvas chair & gawked

at the world of his choosing.

Teal lips with hint of lime

cross the room & brush against mine,

teal lips of hairless Chihuahuas

& nitro glycerin tectonic plates

about to shift again, about to recalculate

the geometry of existence in one giant snort

from its equestrian nostril,

& that's all there is.

Sorry to say,

but life is one long equestrian snort,

sometimes the size of a flea, sometimes

the size of a manatee.

Homesick

Anichka relaxed against a wall of broken plaster and let her eyes trace pendulum shadows back and forth across the floor. The electric lantern hanging over her head swayed in breeze from open windows, spilling a drunken undulation of light about the walls of the room. She bunched up her black waitress apron with one hand and adjusted her short black hair with the other. She smiled at me and tossed her apron to the floor, briefly fingering a chrome stud in her upper lip. The swaying dimness of the lantern cast an odd light on her slightly masculine cheekbones, and the summer sweat of her brow glistened in the moonlight. The river flowed ceaselessly below, and I couldn't help but hang dizzily out the window and watch.

I gripped my half-empty rum bottle hard in my sweaty palm, feeling some security there, security from the spinning room, from my unstoppable vertigo. The noise of the bar drifted up through the floors in a dull roar, but it was all soothingly distant now, as if it misted in from another world.

Anichka fidgeted in the half-light of this unfinished room; the tattoo on her arm—a nautilus shell marked "POMPEII BABY!" in looping script—moved in and out of shadow. I never asked her what it meant, and until now I never bothered to wonder.

"How much are they renovating?" I asked her, forgetting the tattoo and rapping my knuckles on a stretch of cedar window trimming. "This doesn't look original."

She shrugged. "I don't know. I never came up here before they started."

There was just the faintest ghost of her mother tongue in her voice, noticeable only in her rounded Slavic vowels. Her voice—that accent—seemed the only souvenir of her childhood in Donets'k, an atavistic ripple of something she herself could barely recall.

"When are they supposed to finish?" I said, sweeping my arms across the ancient brick and plaster vista, the torn-up fourth story of a century-old warehouse, which stretched maybe twenty-five feet down one axis and some forty-and-change down the other. This walled-up desert of flapping plastic, discarded ladders, rotten support beams, exposed insulation—someday soon it would be a million-dollar condo. But now it was only a blackened mess, lighted sporadically by whichever construction lamps we managed to find.

Anichka shrugged.

"Who knows. No more money, no investors." She smiled impishly at me. "Did you want to move in here?"

"I already live here," I mumbled, not without mirth, as I stared down at the plywood planks, imagining the bar on the first floor. Its noise pummeled the soles of my shoes, my ankles, my knees. Downstairs, the world was delirious and sick and impassioned, but up here there were only the dregs. For a moment I thought I was going to be ill.

"I don't know what they were thinking." She seemed to ignore me. "The developers, I mean."

"About the condos?" The conversation suddenly eluded me. My mind, mired and waterlogged, grappled uselessly with Anichka's words.

"Yeah. Who would pay a million dollars to live in a warehouse?" Those Slavic vowels again. I tried to remember what she was talking about. "Or a mill. Or factory. Whatever this place was."

"Warehouse," I mumbled, half-hoping she didn't hear me.

"A real house would be cheaper," she continued, "even on the water. Who would live here?"

"I don't know." I shrugged and took a drink; the rush of liquor had my stomach turning once more. "Maybe the same people who like to drink here."

"But the bar is nice."

"The condos will be, too." I offered her my bottle. "Rum?"

She took a couple healthy swigs.

"Maybe," she said, wiping her mouth and returning the bottle. "But I still don't get it."

"Wait 'til it's finished, I guess." I clapped her on the shoulder, though I wasn't sure why. She didn't seem to mind, and instead only smiled, tugging my jacket sleeve and leading me across the emptied room. The westernmost wall was full of windows, though many were paneless and had only flapping tarpaulin to keep the elements out.

"I like the view here," she said.

I crept up next to her and stared out the window at the harbor below. A multitude of little candy-colored boats bobbed up and down in the limpid tide, and the black water was narcotic with quicksilver reflections. I swayed where I stood and clasped a hand around Anichka's arm for warmth.

"Feeling okay?" she said, smiling bemusedly and suppressing a little laugh.

"I'm sick," I muttered, struggling to maintain my footing, though I wanted nothing more than to collapse on the dusty planks and pass out. Yet I continued staring at the boats, which still rolled on in chant of the wind, in pools of mumbling ripples that addled the peaceful river. On this troubled surface starry reflections skittered about like electric waterbugs. "I'm sick."

"Poor little boy," Anichka said, tossing an arm around my shoulder with patronizing glee. "Too much medicine?"

"Cheap rum," I said, hoisting the bottle and sliding out of her grip.

She turned; the moonlight caught her arm and I found myself staring at her nautilus tattoo. I wanted to say something about it, but everything I thought of seemed stupid so I kept quiet.

I took another swallow from the rum and offered the bottle to Anichka. She waved it away and lit a cigarette instead.

"Want one?"

"Sure."

She gave me two, and I smoked them down to the filter as quickly as I could. For some reason I felt that I should hurry.

"Do you have a boat?" Anichka suddenly asked, gazing down at the harbor.

I laughed. "You serious?"

"Sure, why not?"

"I get seasick," I said, shrugging. "I shouldn't even be looking at the water."

"I wanna ride on a boat," she mumbled, likely to herself, as she flicked a cigarette butt out the window, into the breeze. "Or maybe go for a swim."

I shrugged again. The room seemed darker now, though I wasn't sure how. The lights we'd turned on were still aglow, but the black of all the nooks and corners almost seemed to be spreading out like some kind of oil slick. Yet the moonlight on Anichka's face was brighter, bluer, more dreamlike.

"You know," I started, struggling hard to recall what I was about to say, "my grandfather was a sailor." I ran a hand through my hair and wiped the sweat from my brow. "Saw the whole world twice over before he was my age."

Anichka nodded and gave me another cigarette. I took a few puffs and stared into the night sky, thinking of ancient sailors, centuried mariners forced to read their existence only by constellations and lunar phases, godly maps that, to them, were surely more real than the dull planks of the ships they sailed, more real than any terrestrial notions of home and family.

And now, leaning against a windowpane in this half-finished warehouse room, staring down at a puny fleet of boats in a black river harbor, I realized I'd never felt so tethered in my life.

"For fuck's sake," I murmured, "I gotta get outta here."

"What?" For the first time all night, her concern seemed genuine.

I shook my head and went to take another drag from my cigarette, but it was no longer in my hand. I bent down and groped about the dirty floor, but I didn't see it anywhere.

"What?" Anichka repeated.

"Lost my cigarette."

"What cigarette?"

"The one you just gave me a minute ago," I grumbled, frustrated. There was nothing on the floor but dust and a couple bent nails, so I brushed my hands on my pants and gave up. I took a step back and saw that I'd crushed what was left of the butt beneath my shoe.

Anichka was quiet now, ignoring me and looking up at the purple sky. Behind us a sheet of tarpaulin flapped in the breeze like a mainsail. I felt faint and, closing my eyes, fell limp against the windowpane. The world washed about me in delirious cascades, and I felt too weak and dizzy to move.

I uncapped the rum, swallowed what remained in a few gulps, and let the bottle slip away from my sweaty fingers. It hit the floor with a dull, reverberating thud, and for a moment I could just barely hear the friction of its spinning.

I'd already opened my mouth to ask Anichka for another cigarette when I noticed that she was gone. For a moment I feared that I'd only imagined her, but that was silly: where else could those cigarette ashes on the floor have come from? So I leaned against the windowframe and waited for her to come back. I watched the sway of a naked yellow lightbulb hanging just behind me. The shifting light threw repeating shadows down the floorplanks, regular as the tide, as if I were cowering in the hull of an old sailing ship.

The moon glowed heavy and mercurial over the water, and I stared dumbly at its echoing and melting reflections on the river. An eternity of water waited only a quarter mile north, though it was invisible from here. I counted the dragon points of the moon along the current instead, idly wondering where Anichka had gone.

She was back a moment later, returning so quietly that I didn't hear her footsteps. She sidled up next to me and waved another bottle in front of my face, grinning.

"More rum?" I sputtered, not really interested.

"Expensive rum," she said. "Grabbed it from the bar. No more of that rotgut you've been drinking."

I smiled, bewildered and dizzy, and nodded some kind of thanks.

"How are you feeling?" she asked, offering me another cigarette.

"Like shit," I muttered, grabbing the rum from her outstretched arm and taking a couple healthy swallows. The world howled relentlessly at me from all directions, and I hoped the glug of the bottle might drown it out. "I'm sick."

Vertigo blew in through one of the empty windows and forced me down to the floor; I didn't resist. I went limp on the planks and shut my eyes, hoping that I could steady the constant nausea that was heaving my stomach into my chest cavity and back again. Now more than ever I felt like a forgotten stowaway on a storm-pitched vessel.

Anichka kicked me in the ribs. "Get up," she said. "You know better than this."

"Fuck you."

I extended an arm and let her drag me back to my feet. I wobbled and supported myself against the windowpane, squinting hard to see whether or not she was smiling. She wasn't.

With my eyes half closed, I watched a fly spiral toward the lightbulb and bounce off its glass with a little plink. I felt a sudden sting at my fingers. A cigarette had burned low enough to singe my hand, but I didn't remember lighting it, or even holding it. I flicked the thing away, cursed, shook the ash from my fingertips.

I stared at the river. Next to me Anichka sighed and put a hand on my back with startling tenderness. She didn't say anything, and withdrew her hand a few seconds later.

The stars were meaningless in the river, indecipherable. I thought of my old mariners again, thought of their star-maps and unimaginable voyages, thought of how they'd carved their memories and mythologies onto the stars, how the strange geometries of constellations were little more than cave paintings in the sky, painted at an impossible scale.

Anichka was pacing around the empty space now, and for a few seconds I concentrated on the spiraling echo of her footsteps on the floorboards. She'd left the rum with me, so I took a few more swallows and wandered over to the center of the room.

Soon I felt the dizzying spin of the world in all its terrifying primacy, and a moment later I was on the floor again, though I couldn't tell if I'd set myself there on purpose or merely fallen. I still clutched the rum in my right hand, though the bottle was unstopped and draining. The liquid drained down the floorboards in little rivulets and slow rivers, dribbled into the spaces between each hunk of wood, soaked into my suit jacket.

I felt Anichka's hands creeping across my body, working at my belt. I stared up at one of the dull lightbulbs at the rafters, and the longer I looked the more it resembled a swollen yellow moon, and its dust a universe of stars. I tried impressing upon it all my private cosmologies and geometries, but the dust was too agitated by the wind.

Anichka had my belt undone and was tugging my pants around my hips. I glanced up at the light and dust again, but somehow it hurt my head to look. I blinked my eyes and tried to pace my breathing, wishing I hadn't spilled the rum.

Anichka's head bobbed in my lap, though I was too numb and limp from the booze to really feel anything. She gave up only a moment later and sighed heavily.

The air in this unfinished warehouse room, though well ventilated, was oppressive somehow, heavy with the weight of the sky, the million pinprick gravities of all its planets. This celestial burden was nearly audible—musical, even—and I felt powerless to do anything but listen.

Anichka's footsteps banged out restless spirals through the dust and shadow, receded, and then were gone. I stayed on the floor, motionless in some sort of starry languor, and imagined the river. I thought of its reflections, though I couldn't tell if the waters reflected the moon or merely an old warehouse lightbulb.

I let out a long sigh and waited for Anichka to come back, patting my jacket for a cigarette.

What You Bring Along

You drove in long bursts from Arizona
toward the sharp New England coastline,
truck bed stacked with nested furniture;
boxes of bromeliads tucked one against
the other, roots secure within their tight-packed
bark enclosures; the kitchen set,
newspaper-separated, eggshell blue,
all tethered against the rattles
and jolts of the road.

The land poured out ahead, pale and shapeless,
edges of the plains dipping into a vague
shadow-haze, and when Ohio gave way
to the green and violet rise of West Virginia,
you were struck by its contours,
the assertive three-dimensionality of it all.

There had been too much sun —
everything yellow and white, scraped raw.
The East was heavy and damp, storms pushing
through with a resonant grind, plumping
the streets into streams and then dissipating,
echoing far along the macadam
and in between the houses' water-swollen shingles.

And somewhere, south of your intended route,
there was a trail bordering a reservoir,
parallel to the attenuated deer-path
and leading down to a point, naked
but for a mat of neon-bright moss
and thin maples.

Crossing the Berkshires, your ears remembered
the gravelly tramp of feet stepping in unison there,
synthetic jackets squeaking against branches,
and the picnic quilt, mothball-tinged,
spreading out along the underbrush, scattering
the sparrows as it unfolded beneath a puzzle
of hand-sized leaves, safe from the rain.

Fingerprint

It was morning and Gwen had never been one to sleep in. She turned on her side taking a deep breath and looked at the boy who slumbered with his face buried in a satin white pillow. Intertwined strands of long, brown hair shielded his face from the dawn. Like her, he was barely twenty; unlike her, he was still too young to understand he was anything more than a boy.

Sunlight peered in and tattooed the white window blinders across the butterscotch bed. Gwen pressed her left hand against the boy's barren back above the line of the bed sheet and absorbed the quiet ups and downs of his breathing. She pressed her lips against one of his shoulder blades and kissed, a slow and full sort of kiss. And when she released, it was as if a small burst of fire transferred from her lips into him. She rose barefoot on a pastel oriental rug. Her body, slender and firm, was nude save for the thin lines of her yellow panties. Thick chestnut coils of hair fell just above her shoulders and made her eyes greener than they really were.

She tucked her hair behind her ears and tied it in a bun. Loose strands fell against the base of her neck. Then she put on a pair of white shorts and a sleeveless green top. The pads of her fingertips brushed gently along the molding of the doorway as she sauntered out onto the crimson carpeted hallway.

Gwen went down the winding stairwell. She grabbed the wooden banister as she turned off the last step and onto the black and white checkered marble of the foyer then through a hallway underneath the stairway.

The kitchen was spacious and bright. Morning light swept in through the large windows and wide, sliding glass doors that led out to the patio. Long white lamps hung from the ceiling. The tin accent of the ceiling and the white of the cabinets contrasted the dark brown color. The floor boards were coarse to her bare feet.

The big island in the center had a faucet on one side and long legged chairs on the opposite. Their backs basked in the warmth of light and the dark upholstery of the chairs matched the island's brown top. She leaned a hand on the smooth counter top and felt a sensation in the depths of her belly.

It was a sort of tingling, piercing pain that made her think she was incomplete. It made her long for something intangible. She pressed a hand against the source, not in the attempt to fight the sensation but rather to spread it throughout her body. It did not mean she wanted this feeling. In fact, it unnerved her. She caught her muted reflection in the window and hoped the sensation was thirst or the occasional morning cramp. The other possibility was too frightening to consider.

Gwen filled a pot with water and placed it on the front right burner. Instead of knobs and dials on the side, the stove had small keypads; one for each burner and the oven underneath. Each keypad was numbered 1 through 9 with another button labeled "on/off". The keypad for the oven utilized an extra button labeled "start".

A paper was hastily taped on the oven window. Different degrees of heat were assigned to the different numbers. For the burners, 1 was labeled abstractly as "Least". "Very Hot" was assigned to 7 and "Really Hot" corresponded to 8. She smiled, thinking that "Really" and "Very" could just as easily be switched around with no effect on the result. She pressed the 8 on the keyboard for the front right burner. The button stayed pressed and blue flames judged up. That an otherwise slick and expensive stove had been so clunkily outfitted was testament to Mary; that the alterations worked was testament to the boy's genius.

In a few minutes, the pot whistled and Gwen repressed the 8, pushing it out and killing the flames. She got out honey, chamomile tea, and two cups from the cabinets above and laid a thick layer of honey in both cups. Next, the tea leaves were put in and the water was poured. She breathed in the heat and the aroma.

She heard the front door open and leaned back to find a middle aged woman in a flowery dress and small blonde ponytail walk in. The woman plopped a phone on the foyer table.

"Good morning, Gwen!" she called into the kitchen.

Gwen waved at her, "Good morning, Mrs. Hagliff!"

"I told you, you're spending enough time here, Mary…please."

"Okay... Mary." Gwen still hadn't gotten used to that.

"That's better," Mary said as she went back outside. Through the open door, Gwen made out a silver Mercedes parked at an angle. Mary opened a back door and began unloading a couple of bags. The cobblestone driveway stretched from the house gates and curved before the front door went back to the gate. In its middle was a vibrant flower garden.

"Mary, want a hand with those?"

"Absolutely!"

Gwen pulled the front door shut and went down to the car. "I don't know anyone else who shops at ten in the morning."

"Gwen, I don't shop at ten. I get there when the farmers set up at around seven!"

Gwen chuckled, "Oh, okay then!"

They each picked up a pair of bags and headed toward the door. Following, Gwen said, "By the way, love the dress!"

"Thank you, honey!" Mary said turning her head back, "see that's why I need another woman around here."

They reached the door. "Gwen can you swipe your thumb, please?" Mary nodded toward a clunky black box attached the wall on their right ride. Thin, blue lines ran horizontally inside a concave in the middle of the box.

Gwen laid the bags on the granite patio and swiped. The screen above the concave read "denied" in a digital font.

"Sorry. My print's not registered," Gwen said.

"Not possible. The boy's already gone for you."

Mary's response took Gwen by surprise. Nevertheless, a faint smile formed on her lips.

"Swipe again, honey."

Again, the screen read: denied.

"No keys?" Gwen asked instinctively.

"Not anymore." Mary drew Gwen's attention down to the doorknob, whose keyhole was covered up with masking tape. "Let me try." Mary sat her bags down and swiped. The screen flashed "denied".

"Phone?"

"In the foyer. You?"

"Upstairs. We can honk," Gwen suggested, hinting with her eyes at the car.

Mary headed to the car and honked a couple times. They waited a few minutes but there was no indication Krim heard. Mary got out of the car and approached Gwen. "No luck. The house is pretty much sound proof."

Gwen stood on her tiptoes and looked in through a square glass window atop the door. So close, yet so far away.

"See Gwen? Instead of compliments I get technology that makes my life harder. This is why I need you around."

"Well, the stove works, at least." She came back down on her heels.

"Until today so did the scanner."

"We could try the back door."

"That has a scanner, too. But it's worth a shot," Mary decided and Gwen followed as they went down the steps, turned off the cobbled driveway, onto a granite walkway that led them through another flower garden, this one of roses and lilies, before reaching the backyard. They went up a wooden patio and came to a slide glass door.

Mary swiped a thumb on the box to her left. The screen read "denied" in the same familiar font as before.

"At least he linked them together properly?" Gwen suggested.

"Krim still sleeping?"

"Yeah."

"Figures."

"I made breakfast but didn't want to wake him," Gwen said.

Mary glanced at her with a look that was almost solemn. The look triggered Gwen to say, "I'm sorry? Did I say something wrong?"

"No. no," Mary shook her head and proceeded to sit in one of the chairs around the steel patio table. "Nothing sweetie. Just hadn't realized it before. Come. Sit." Mary invited Gwen to have a sit.

"Realized what?" Gwen pulled out the next chair over which offered a view into the kitchen behind Mary's shoulder.

"You're in love with my son."

The words hit Gwen like a punch in the gut. She froze for a moment, contemplating. Mary only showed a delicate smirk.

"I couldn't possibly." Gwen finally pulled the chair in.

"You could. And you are."

Gwen tucked loose strands of hair behind her ears and leaned forward. "Look, Mary, if it's about breakfast: it was only cereal."

"Bet you didn't pour the milk."

There was silence. Mary folded her arms and leaned back. Then said, "And the pit of your stomach, those aren't cramps."

Gwen buried her face in her hands, succeeding in hiding her grin but failing miserably to disguise her chuckle.

"Don't worry. Krim's like a leech. He grows on people."

After regaining control, Gwen looked up and said, "I think Krim just likes me. That's all."

"No," she leaned in, put her forearms on the punctured steel pattern of the table, "for all his gadgetry, long hair, and lack of polo shirts, Krim is a sole heir..."

"I have no interest in using him, Mary," Gwen said with a tone the mixture of blunt and stern.

"And I'm not trying to insinuate otherwise. My point is Krim's background makes him very sought after," she swirled her fingers in the air and with her eyes drew Gwen's attention to their surroundings of gated, spacious houses drenched in ornate gardens. "For every girl

34

around here. When it comes to him, they are all single. Yet, you're the only one he's cared for enough to spend nights here with."

Gwen said nothing. Her eyes rolled down to the table. Unbeknownst to her, she saw her index finger tracing a circular patch of the crisscross design.

Mary continued, "In other words, all of this is his greatest tragedy, Gwen." Mary's mention of her name brought Gwen's eyes level with Mary's. "The door lock problem aside, Krim is a prodigy. But whatever he accomplishes in life will be severely discounted by posterity - if not disqualified altogether. If he has a saving grace, it's that he really doesn't give a damn about others' opinions of him." Then with an augury point of the finger at Gwen, "And I think you don't give a damn, either."

Through the glass panel, Gwen noticed Krim walk into the kitchen. His hand swept back long strands from his face.

"There he is!" she raised an arm up and motioned Krim to open the door.

Mary turned to see her son stop and pour hot water into a cup before walking toward them. Then she checked her watch and turned to Gwen, "Only ten twenty. Didn't think it possible."

The door slid open and Krim stepped half out, "Thanks for the tea, whoever."

Mary looked over at Gwen, "You didn't mention the tea."

" 'preciate it Gwen," Krim leaned back in.

"Don't you dare!" Mary stopped him in his tracks and rose to her feet, "your contraption doesn't work."

"Not possible," he replied.

"Oh, very factual, actually," she prompted him to try himself, passing by him on her way in.

Krim, his feet still inside the kitchen, leaned out and swiped a thumb. The screen recalled its "denied" message.

"Hmm."

"Hmm's not good enough, Krim. I want it working in five or we're back to lock and key!" She called passing through the kitchen.

"Good morning, sugar." Gwen pecked him on the cheek, caressing a hand along his jaw as she stepped inside. She followed Mary through the kitchen. Leaving the kitchen and entering the hall, the tingle in her abdomen returned and she pressed the same hand against it. When she glanced back, she found only Krim's silhouette stretched on the patio floor boards as he studied the contraption and she hoped the sensation would last a long, long time.

The Original Sin & The Blasphemous Blues

Here is everything blue and golden and here is where morning meets afternoon and the in-between evades, nothing for breakfast but swallowed words and guilt-free conversations beneath dripping reds and the violent crashing clanging of inner monologue and four letter words. Imagine, create. Action, reaction. Infectious dialogue pollutes the air and so I'm keeping my lips sealed, my tongue tied. All originality disappeared with the invention of the wheel and you're saying That was my idea, first, No, this just isn't fair. And I'm telling you Honestly, a liar's tongue tastes just as sweet no truthful lips could hope to compare, here is everything blue and golden, here is where morning meets afternoon.

Just a Patch of Grass

My Uncle Jack never had a wife or kids and I never had a father. He was a large man with a thin face and skinny legs, an unnaturally large stomach, a result of rich helpings and drink. Uncle Jack had a young face, the kind of face that looked like he had never worked a day in his life, small wrinkles around his eyes only visible when he smiled, usually after telling a dirty joke that made men laugh, that is, until, the glare of their wives stopped them .

While my mother worked as a receptionist. I spent summers with Uncle Jack. He'd give me a list of chores to complete during the day and we'd sit on the deck and talk sports, girls, and boats until the sun went down. I remember how he'd sip his beer and lean back, staring at the sun, his head propped on top of the chair like he was getting his hair washed at the barber shop. He had the kind of voice that took control of a room, experience gained from years as a court attorney. "You fellas heard the one about the one-legged girl?" he asked at the last family reunion. The wives groaned, one of them mumbling, "I guess that's our cue," and walked away. "Glad they left," Uncle Jack said, "Because I forgot the punchline!" Then he reached into the cooler for a beer, the sunlight glaring off the aluminum can. That was the last time I saw Uncle Jack.

He died a few months later. Cancer, the doctor said. Untreatable. "I'm surprised you didn't feel anything sooner," the doctor said during Uncle Jack's first visit. I sat with him in the examination room. Uncle Jack's fortune from being an injury claims lawyer in Key West was divided between his two brothers and sister, my mother, my cousins, and me. He left money for everyone else, six figures, not an even number for anyone. My mother's got $235,369.36. Everyone spent time comparing their numbers, trying to find a hidden meaning, figuring out why someone got more and someone else got less, but I think ole' Uncle Jack was just messing with them, knowing the money'd be blown before he was cold in the grave. He left his speedboat to me, Jack's Shack, a custom red and black Apache. He always let me drive it while he sipped a beer and watched the way the water divided in our wake, always telling me to "let her breathe." When we'd pull into the dock, he'd say, "Let's not tell anyone about you driving today."

"We need a swing set," Julie, my wife, said. We sat in our backyard in the early morning, sipping coffee and reading the paper before Andy, our six year-old, woke up. The sun peeked through the row of pines, the shadows on the grass resembling a skewed checkerboard.

I surveyed the backyard for the thousandth time. I knew Julie wouldn't let it go, relying on the "I had a swing set when I was a kid" argument. No matter how many times I told her Andy would turn out normal with or without a swing set, that the park was a bike's ride away, she persisted. "Where would it go?" I asked, already knowing the answer.

Julie stared at the boat to her right, its elevated nose poking out where the house ended. "There would be perfect," she said, pointing in the general direction of the boat. I sighed. "Where's the boat going?"

Julie lifted both hands, palms outward, and shrugged.

"I'm not selling it, if that's what you're suggesting."

"I'm going to check on Andy," she said. She left the table with her coffee, a sure sign she wasn't coming back.

I walked to the side of the boat and surveyed it. It was a thirty-footer, stretching the entire length of the house and then some. The tires from the trailer killed the grass it sat on, the boat doing the rest, blocking the grass from the sun. The speed boat hadn't moved in seven years, its only trip a quick jut around Cape Cod during a vacation. Ever since Julie got pregnant, she'd deemed the boat too dangerous, claiming I wasn't experienced enough to drive it. It didn't help that we lived in Utica, New York, at least four hours from the closest beach. Mr. Windsor, our neighbor, told me on more than one occasion that the "piece of shit I have to look at every morning when I'm taking a dump" has to go." I told Julie if the boat is blocking us from being in the living room and seeing Mr. Windsor crap, that should settle it. She didn't laugh, instead agreeing that it was sore on the eyes and an imposition on our elderly neighbors.

I let Andy use the boat with his friends when they came over, even got him a captain hat he could use. Andy and his friends would stand in the boat and take turns steering the wheel making "vroom-vroom" noises, ducking when imaginary waves hit. Julie said even that was too dangerous, since the kids could fall getting out. Andy and his friends could only use it when she was out grocery shopping.

Julie was reading the newspaper at the kitchen table when I walked in, my coffee gone, stomach rumbling. I poured cereal and sat on the couch in the family room, watching sports highlights. I let Rocket, our golden lab, lick the milk from my cereal bowl.

"Don't let him do that," Julie said from the kitchen. "That's gross."

"That's what a dishwasher's for. The milk's just gonna go to waste."

"Is Rocket drinking from one of your bowls again?" Andy asked. He rubbed his eye as he walked down the steps in his pajamas. His curly brown hair was a mess.

"I'll make you some scrambled eggs," Julie said. She folded the newspaper and placed it on the corner of the kitchen table. Andy sat at the table, petting Rocket.

"You sleep well?" I asked.

"You know," Julie started. "We owe another thousand dollars in taxes for that stupid boat. That's around seven thousand dollars we've paid in taxes since we inherited that mess."

"It's covered," I said.

"We don't have that kind of money. Andy needs new shoes, you just bought another suit for work, and I have to get my transmission fixed. Where's that thousand dollars coming from?"

"We'll take care of it."

Julie slammed the spatula on the frying pan, the hard clank startling Andy and Rocket. She stirred the eggs furiously in tense, tight movements. Raw egg spilled over the side of the pan and onto the floor, chunks of egg debris speckling the linoleum. Rocket sprinted over and began licking it. "You know that thousand dollars could be going towards a swing set? Towards growing the grass back? Towards not being the laughingstock of the neighborhood, looking like a family of rednecks with a huge boat and nowhere to use it?"

"We could always rent it out. I'm sure someone in Utica would love to say they live on a boat. I don't know how the bathroom situation would work..."

"I've had it," Julie said, walking upstairs, leaving the eggs sizzling in the pan. Andy stared out the window, his expression silent. I finished cooking his eggs, the outer layer firm but not yet brown.

"Are you getting rid of Uncle Jack's boat?" Andy asked between mouthfuls of eggs. He always referred to the boat as Uncle Jack's because I always did.

"I hope not," I said. "I love that boat."

"Me too," Andy said. "I'm the only kid in school with a boat."

"I know."

As Andy finished his eggs, Julie came downstairs and grabbed her keys off the counter. "Andy, I have to run some errands," she said. Julie wore her sunglasses, which I thought looked silly indoors. She wore one of her flowered yellow and blue sundresses, her brown hair pulled back into a ponytail. "I'll be back, all right?" She kissed him on the forehead and left, the door slamming behind her.

"I think she's mad at you, Dad."

"Let's run some of our own errands."

* * *

It had been years since I'd hooked the trailer up to the car. After securing the attachment, I started the car, Andy in the passenger seat. I pressed the gas, felt no movement, the engine straining. Finally after flooring the gas pedal, I felt a lurch. The car jolted forward with the boat, probably leaving huge divots in the grass. I didn't look back.

"What are we doing with the boat, Dad?" Andy asked.

"We're gonna take her out, let her breathe."

We rode in silence, Andy's head pressed against the window as signs flew past. I checked the rearview mirror frequently to see if the boat was still attached. My fingers tapped the steering wheel.

I followed signs for the Long Island Sound. I rolled down Andy's window. "Smell that breeze, son?"

"I'm hungry."

I followed the signs for Wilson's Cove. Uncle Jack always kept Jack's Shack at his harbor, and I needed help maneuvering the boat off the trailer. Andy and I stood as the workers backed the trailer into the water and unhitched the boat. The younger of the two filled the boat with gas.

"Gonna have to be back by six if you want some help reattaching the trailer," the older man said. He looked to be in his 60s, his face golden brown, strands of white hair covering bald spots.

"I can get it myself," I said.

The man looked at me, then at Andy. "Okay," he said. "Just leave your keys with Bobby and we'll square up when you get back. Do you have your own life jackets or you gonna need a couple?"

I pretended to look in the trunk, knowing damn well I'd forgotten them. "Don't seem to have them with me."

* * *

"This is awesome!" Andy screamed as I goosed the throttle. Jack's Shack sliced through the gentle waves, leaving behind a foamy wake. Splashes of salt water sprayed our faces. The engine purred like it was making up for lost time, for the past seven years being nothing but a giant lawn decoration.

We had the ocean to ourselves. Andy and I took turns steering the wheel. I had to hold him so he'd be able to see over the windshield, his eyes fixed on the water in front of him, his tongue poking out as he concentrated. "Let's not tell anyone about you driving today," I said, mussing Andy's hair.

"Okay," he said.

I drove Jack's Shack back to the marina. As we approached, I sounded the horn to signal Bobby. No one came from the small shop. Andy and I floated for five minutes, watching, waiting.

"Maybe he's gone, Dad," Andy said.

"I think so," I said, gently pressing the throttle.

"Don't you need help getting it on the trailer?"

"That's what you're for," I said. I brought Jack's Shack as close to the dock as I could and hoisted Andy onto the wooden planks before climbing out myself. I backed the trailer into the water as Andy watched from the dock, his hands on his hips, a serious expression across his face.

"I'm bringing her in slow," I told Andy. He nodded his understanding. I pressed the throttle down, felt the boat jolt forward. The gentle ripples pushed Jack's Shack towards the trailer in a slow drift. The setting sun reflected off the nose.

"Maybe a little more gas," Andy said.

I pressed down on the throttle, hearing the engine purr back to life. As soon as I heard the engine, I knew it was too much. The boat lurched forward. The hull of Jack's Shack met the trailer with a grinding screech as it entered the trailer crookedly. I was afraid of the nose going through the back window of the car. I managed to keep my balance, holding onto the steering wheel. Andy had a look of horror on his face, and I knew from looking at him that Jack's Shack wasn't looking too good. There was no way for me to get the boat off the trailer without causing more damage.

Sharp pain shot through my knee as I jumped from the boat to the dock.

"I don't think we're getting her down, bud," I said, hands on my hips.

"No," Andy said.

We sat on the dock and stared at the boat, our bare feet swishing on the water.

"Are you and Mom going to get a divorce?" Andy asked.

"No, of course not."

"Okay," Andy said, staring at his feet. "It's just that you guys fight a lot."

"I know. We need to work on that," I said, mussing Andy's hair. "As hard as it is to believe, Dad's not perfect." Despite the boat's condition, a smile crept onto my face. "Let me unhook this trailer so we can get home."

"What about the boat?"

"I'll see what I can do tomorrow. It's not looking too good though." I ran my hand under the boat, the metal scratches cutting deep into Jack's Shack.

As we pulled out of the lot, the nose of the boat grew smaller in front of the setting sun. I kept my eyes on the rearview mirror until I turned the corner onto the road.

* * *

Andy slept most of the ride home. He didn't budge when I pulled into our driveway. His body was limp with exhaustion when I extracted him from his seatbelt and pulled him close to my chest, surprised at how heavy he'd gotten. Julie was downstairs watching TV. I put my index finger to my mouth, pointing with my head to Andy. I laid him face down on his bed, took off his shoes, and pulled the covers up to his shoulders. I kissed his forehead and shut the door.

"You could have left a note," Julie said from the couch.

"I didn't know where you were going either. We were just taking the boat out for a spin."

"I knew you were doing something stupid like that."

"It was a beautiful day," I said. I reached into the refrigerator and took out a beer. "I'll be outside," I said, opening the patio door, feeling the cool breeze caress my neck. I sat in my chair and propped my feet on Julie's chair and leaned my head back like Uncle Jack. I felt a slight shiver, the night chill a reminder that summer was not yet here.

Seagulls Marching Before the Tide

big big sadness you live in

comes out and says

Not Now and Maybe Never

like you haven't met them

undone I exist beyond

bits of bud and eye of pollen

generously gendered and air-railed

(aural mist lifting its tentative engine

from grass throats and avian tinnitus)

bigger than the box I put big in

to hold it in my possibles

nobody knows me inside myself but

something horrible for a while now

what interests me is not me

it's the place where I am

when I'm not here

I tell the bird not to open itself

but it has me to absent welcome

feathered being-warmth

that means no return

such as involuntary rocks for example

or the war there is swept inward

and not released until the sand lifts

towards shore and separates salt water

greens and tears open

a succession of ancient pacing we refer to as renewal

The Sweet Smell of Pine Needles

The bar's closing. Is it really that late?

Damn. Elizabeth won't like this. She sends me to the bar so she can have some time to herself, but the bar sends me right back to her. Third night this week I've been here. It's not my favorite place in the world but I seem to end up here a lot. This time, I've only been here for seven hours; when she kicked me out today, I got the impression that this time, she was thinking more in terms of years. Elizabeth, Elizabeth, my Elizabeth

The clean smell of gin rises from underneath my collar, a pleasant smell, like pine needles -- so sweet, now, in the summertime! Gin smells like pine needles, that's what Dad used to say and the older I get and the more gin I drink, the more I realize Dad was so right. I only drink the good stuff, the Bombay Sapphire. That bottle looks so pretty and bright blue up there on the shelf, beaming at you, waiting for you, saying *kiss me kiss me kiss me*. Some people say it's all the same going down -- poison is poison, no matter how pretty it is or how sweet it smells like pine needles -- but let me tell you, no. Bombay Sapphire smells like the very best pine needles, what a good blue gin and tonight I have drunk quite a lot of good blue gin that smells like the best pine needles and so now I smell like pine needles, too.

But Elizabeth does not like pine needles. I can't tell you why, but she doesn't. I would think she would enjoy a good whiff of pine needles better than anybody. She's gotten her share over the years, God knows. On my collar, on my breath, on my coat, in the carpet where I puked and she had to clean up after me.

I want another drink. Is it really too much to ask for just one more drink before this shitty bar closes? What a dump. Dark. Unclean. I hear water dripping behind the walls no really I swear I do. Why the hell do I hang out here? The glasses on the bar look like they need to be washed again. These old wooden stools look like dangerous rickety. I remember when they were new. They felt almost comfortable back in those days. A man could sit on one and not feel like he'd get thrown in the floor if he leaned too far in one direction.

Now they need some paint. Maybe some fresh leather padding. Maybe just a new cushion, something in a happier color, purple maybe. Royal Purple like a king's crown, not purplish black like a bruise.

I raise my hand to get the bartender's attention, and notice he's already staring at me. I know what that stare means, don't think I don't know what that stare means. He thinks I'm drunk. Of course, I *am* drunk. But he thinks I'm *too* drunk, that I'm one of those guys that gets his tab and then wads it up and throws it back and maybe takes a haymaker swing at the bartender for good measure. But, the thing is, I'm clearly not one of those guys. Those guys don't wear thousand-dollar suits or diamond-studded Rolexes and don't have laminated business cards that say *Northeastern Bank Vice President, Mortgage Division*, either. No, I'm one of the good guys in this world. And frankly, I don't need those looks from that bartender. What an asshole. Who does he think he is? I come in here a lot; he doesn't need to look at me that way. There's nothing wrong with me. I may be drunk but I'm not an idiot. That bartender *wishes* he could find something wrong with me. He wants to cut me off. He wants a reason to get tough with me, to raise his voice and show the bar who's boss. Fuck him. I got money. I pay my tab in town. I pay a lot of tabs in this town. What's he worried about? Fuck him. He's a bartender, not a babysitter. I'm not a baby here. Asshole.

I raise my hand again, stretch a little higher. I'm a polite drunk. "Hey, man," I say to the asshole. "Can I have another drink, please?" So polite, so civilized, so in control of myself. People ought to be more civilized in this world. I bet none of the other jerks in here are civilized as me.

"Sorry, Gary, you just had last call," says the asshole. "Ready for your tab?"

"Just one more, please," I say.

I wonder why I come here. This clown at the bar doesn't even know who I am he must be new. I should find a new bar. A new bar that appreciates its paying customers. Fuck him. Fuck this bar.

I wonder why I come here.

Pine needles.

Elizabeth.

I met Elizabeth in a Lexington bookstore, a gigantic two-story place called Russo's that had thick maroon carpeting and more books in it than the public libraries of most small American cities. We were both seniors in college. Elizabeth worked at Russo's as a cashier, with a deep love for 18th and 19th century Gothic literature. She was fascinated by novels and poems that I never knew existed, written by authors whose names I'd never heard before she whispered them to me.

My literary tastes, on the other hand, tended to fall into a more contemporary vein: I didn't really like books. People like me, we don't have time for books. But, the hot word around campus held that beautiful and wanting young women wandered the aisles of Russo's in search of all the goods that frat-house guys like me offered in abundance. Sounds dumb now, but I believed it then. And because I believed it, I kept going back there and hanging around in sections where I thought the prettiest girls would be. Poetry, philosophy, self-improvement, art. Don't know why I believed girls were so attracted to poetry, philosophy, self-improvement, or art, but when I first saw Elizabeth she was reading from a thin little book of Spanish poems. So there.

That day, I knew. As the old song says, sometimes a man just knows. I knew this was My Elizabeth. My Elizabeth was tall and thin and blonde, warm and graceful as a spring breeze, and I knew. She had on sandals, loose jeans, and a pink blouse with the ugliest floral pattern I'd ever seen in my life, and she read poetry in a foreign language, and she loved things that I never cared about or knew existed, and still, I knew. My Elizabeth.

I ask again, "Can I have just one more?" but the bartender says, "Gotta close up, Gary. I'll get your tab," and then he looks at me like my nose has just fell off. I don't say anything to him, though I do imagine picking up my glass and throwing it through his forehead. That would be fun. But instead, I shrug my shoulders, pick the glass up from the bar, and finish off my last gulp of gin and tonic.

Gary. He called me Gary. My name is not Gary. He knows my name is Vincent, has known that for God-knows how many years. Normally, I couldn't care less if he remembers my name or not, but now he wants to be all buddy-buddy with me and he can't remember my name and I hate that. He doesn't want to be my friend. I don't want him to be my friend. I'm just an unpaid tab to this guy, and he'll say whatever he thinks he needs to say to get that tab covered and me out the door without incident.

No doubt, he's afraid I'll try and skip out the door or take a swing at him when that check comes. Tonight, I drank twenty-six gin and tonics -- I know because whenever I drink, I place each little black stirrer under my leg, to keep track, to keep from getting screwed -- and maybe if another man drinks twenty-six gin and tonics he might be a load to handle. But I am not like another man. I am me, there's only one of me, I am polite and I am civilized and I've got this under control. I pay my tab, I pay a lot of tabs. Just bring me the bill so I can get out of here.

I reach for my wallet. It's thick with cash, more cash than this bartender makes in two months. And he thinks I won't pay my bill. Right.

The asshole brings the bill back to my end of the bar. "How much?" I say, taking the little white slip of paper from his hand before he can lay it down on the bar in front of me. I hate when they lay the tab face-down on the bar. It's like they're ashamed of the dollar amount. So rude -- do they think I don't know exactly how much I drank? Guys like me, we always know the bill, not that it really matters, not that there's ever a danger we can't cover it.

"Thanks, Gary," he says. "I'll take it when you're ready. We close in ten minutes, okay?" Then he walks away again. I start to yell after him, start to inform him that I'm not Gary, I'm Vincent, I don't know Gary, shut up about Gary. But instead, I just check the tab, pull a hundred and twenty-five bucks out of my wallet, then throw in an extra fifty just to show the asshole that I can. Then I leave.

The day before our tenth wedding anniversary, Northeastern promoted me to *Vice President, Mortgage Division*. I'd worked a lot of long nights, made a lot of sacrifices -- seventy hour weeks, no vacation in five years, things like that -- and I deserved the recognition. The same night I got the news, I took Elizabeth to a restaurant downtown that we'd had our eye on for years, but never been able to afford, a strictly jacket-and-tie place on Broadway that was a little fancier than the one we'd planned for our anniversary dinner the next night, but which I thought was more than justified considering the special occasion.

This restaurant was the real deal. The kind of place where a tablecloth might cost more than an average man's suit, where a set of silverware was worth more than all the dishes we had in our house, and where reservations were most definitely required at least two weeks in advance. "But don't worry about that," I said to Elizabeth. "We'll get in." I promised that I would slip the guy in front a hundred dollar bill, get us in that way. We could afford to do things like that now. We could afford to pay what it took to get what we wanted. "Order whatever the hell you want, too. Anything," I said.

When we sat down at our table, I told the waiter to bring the most expensive bottle of cabernet sauvignon in the building. He looked at me funny (I guess people only order that way in movies) but he did as requested. To be honest, I never would have guessed that a single bottle of cabernet sauvignon, even one with such an unpronounceable name on the label, could cost that much. But it was worth it.

While we waited for our meal, I noticed that Elizabeth's gaze kept moving away from me and settling on whoever sat behind me. Finally, I asked, "What are you looking at?"

"What? I'm not looking at anything," she said.

"Are you sure?"

"I'm sure."

"Okay, then," I said. It was such a celebration; I didn't want a fight. I finished my glass of expensive cabernet, and then excused myself to the men's room. As I walked, though, I made a special effort to notice exactly who *was* seated behind me. I saw only a man in a dark brown suit, silver hair, maybe sixty years old. He sat by himself, reading the business pages, circling a few words here and there. The food on his plate was practically untouched.

When I got back to the table, I tried again. "You're sure you don't know that guy?" I asked Elizabeth.

"Which guy?" she said.

"The guy with the newspaper." I motioned towards him.

She looked behind me and shrugged. "Sorry, I don't know him. Why? You think he knows me?" She laughed. I picked up the wine, filled my glass again. I asked Elizabeth if she wanted any more, but she said she'd had enough. Which was fine -- that just left more for me.

That night, we took a cab home because two glasses of wine was too much for Elizabeth, and also because I drank my share of that expensive cabernet sauvignon, then ordered another bottle and drank it all myself. The cab driver was a big fat guy who smelled like a rotten cigar and wore a Green Bay Packers t-shirt that was way too tight around the armpits. When we got to the driveway, Elizabeth asked the cabby if he could help carry me up the steps and into the house. On the way in, I rolled my head over onto his shoulder and puked expensive red wine all over that Packers shirt and also all over the side of the cabby's face, too. He didn't care much for that. Fortunately, though, we were already in the house at that point, and when he dropped me, I landed on the living room couch, which was soft black leather, brand new. Elizabeth gave the man fifty dollars on top of the fare for his troubles and said she was sorry I puked on him, that I got that way sometimes but that was pretty bad even for me. Then she helped me upstairs, undressed me and put me to bed and even kissed me on the forehead.

I remember that kiss. So soft, so warm, so perfect. The world spun and my brain sloshed inside my head like a rubber duck in a bathtub, but I remember that kiss.

"Goodnight, Vincent," I heard Elizabeth say, and then the world went dark.

Sometime in the night, my dreams floated in on an ocean of red wine, dreams I didn't understand, dreams that maybe I didn't want to understand, and yet dreams that, somehow, I never forgot.. I saw so many things in my sleep that night. Business cards, stacked to the stars.

A thousand empty houses, begging me to mortgage them to happy young couples. A solid oak desk, bought just for me, sitting in the middle of an office that was so big I had to take a taxi to get from one side to the other. I saw a fat cab driver in a Green Bay Packers shirt. I saw a bottle of cabernet sauvignon, tall as me, taller than me, the tallest and most expensive bottle of cabernet sauvignon in the whole world. I saw a silver-haired old man in a brown suit, sitting all alone in a restaurant, reading the business pages and circling things that interested him while his food rotted on the plate before him.

And I saw a girl.

A girl, a beautiful girl, tall and thin and blonde, warm and graceful as a spring breeze, wearing sandals, loose jeans, and a pink blouse with the prettiest floral pattern I could ever imagine. She stood in a bookstore. She asked if I liked poetry, and I said no, not really, and then she smiled and said that's fine, poetry isn't really all that important, anyway.

It's a nice night to stagger home drunk.

The warm wind keeps me from passing out on the sidewalk. I welcome the help. Since I walked out of the bar I've ascended three levels of drunkenness. Pine needles sneak up on you.

My house waits ahead. Our house. Her house. I wonder, is Elizabeth still awake? The lights are all turned off. I hope she's still awake. I feel the last seven hours rise out of my stomach, into my throat. Please be awake, Elizabeth. Please God, let her be awake.

I drop to my knees and throw up beside our mailbox.

Ten minutes later, I make it up the steps. I reach for the doorknob and find she's locked the door, but that doesn't make me mad. When you've got as much expensive stuff as we do, you keep the doors locked and the alarm system activated or else you'll wake up one morning and find you made a good Christmas for some sixteen year old shitass thief.

I knock on the door, quiet as I can. Don't want to be too loud, don't want to awaken the neighbors and damn sure don't want to set their damn dogs barking. The neighbors really hate that. I've awakened the neighbors and their damn dogs way too many times before, and the last time I did it they brought up the homeowner's association bylaws and threatened to toss us out of the neighborhood. I don't want to get tossed out of the neighborhood. It's such an expensive neighborhood.

I wait for a light to come on in the window, but no light comes on. I wait for Elizabeth to come and let me in. I wait. I wait. A long time I wait, half an hour, then a whole hour, but she doesn't come and she doesn't let me in. I stand on the porch until two-thirty in the morning, let the warm wind blow in my face, and enjoy the smell that rises from underneath my collar, the wonderful smell to which I have grown so accustomed: the sweet smell of pine needles.

Finally, sometime later but I'm not really sure *what* time, I hear footsteps inside the house. Coming down the stairs, into the living room. A light switches on, the door clicks open, and Elizabeth stands there in front of me. Her eyes are red, swollen, watery. She looks like she hasn't slept in a week. Maybe she hasn't. I think hard, hard as twenty-six gin and tonics will allow me. It's been a few hours since I left the bar but if there's one thing I've learned it's that those pine needles stick to you for a while.

I want to say the right thing. I'm not sure there is a right thing.

"Hello, Elizabeth," I say.

"I thought we agreed," says Elizabeth

She thinks we agreed? Agreed on what?

"You know exactly what, Vincent," Elizabeth says. I realize that I was thinking out loud again. Damn.

But the thing is, I *don't* know what. I never know what. And Elizabeth, she knows that I never know what. She thinks I don't know what because I just don't *want* to know what. Maybe there is some truth to that. I start to apologize, start to say I'm sorry, I don't know what, What? But Elizabeth holds up her hand and stops me. She wipes her puffy red eyes and stares at me for a long time. I don't know how long exactly, just that it's a long time, maybe the longest time we have ever gone like this, staring at each other, silent, unsure.

Then, her gaze jumps and settles on something or someone over my shoulder. I whip my head around, who's she looking at? Then I see him, for a shadowy moment. I see him. The man in the brown suit, the man with the silver hair, the man from our big expensive dinner all those years ago. The man in the brown suit with the newspaper spread out before him, the man who sits alone and quietly circles the interesting parts of the business section. I see him. I see him! What is he doing here now? Here with me, me and Elizabeth, my Elizabeth. I reach for him. I want to know. I am drunk, too drunk. Still I turn from my beautiful Elizabeth, and reach for the man behind me, and open my mouth to ask what he's doing in the darkness, just beyond us. But by then, he's gone.

Immigration

Losses are vacuums
sucking mind out of skull.
They leave cavities of air
that collect dust—
particles I reassemble
to map blueprints—
new languages I learn,
reciting my own name
in hallways of mirrors,
watching *r*'s roll down lips
that memorize pronunciation,
foreign alphabets—
thick accents that confuse
a stranger who stares alone
at an alien's reflection.

The Last Night Out

The tall boy walked into the pawnshop carrying a long, black gun bag. He hadn't yet grown into his bones that seemed to be sticking out like a skeleton with skin hung badly on them. The boy laid the long bag on the counter, under which a hundred watches laid side by side in a locked, glass case. "How much can I get for this?"

The clerk unzipped the bag. "Where did you get it?'"

"My dad gave it to me for my sixteenth birthday. I've never used it."

The man glanced at the boy's long slender fingers and manicured nails. "You don't like hunting?"

"No, I hate it." The boy said it with such vehemence that several men in red, flannel shirts stopped shuffling through merchandise and looked toward the counter.

The clerk pulled the gun out of its leather case. It was a Springfield 3006 rifle, as clean as the day it left the factory. "One hundred"

"That's all?"

"It's a pawn shop," the clerk shrugged.

"But it's brand new."

"You said you got it for your sixteenth birthday. How old are you now?"

"Nineteen." He pulled himself up to his full height.

"So it's three years old."

"But never used." One flannel shirted man poked the boy in the shoulder, "That's too low."

The boy flinched as if he had been hit.

The clerk shot the interloper a dirty look. "Okay, I'll give you one-twenty, but that's it."

The boy shook his head no but shrugged his shoulders and said, "Okay."

The clerk wrote out the paper work and handed over the cash. As he walked out, two men walked up to the counter and said, "Let me look at that gun."

Twenty minutes later, the same young man took two steps into the tailor shop and stopped. He looked around the room filled with women, brushed his dishwater hair out of his hazel eyes and blinked.

"May I help you?" The squat, older woman stood up from her sewing machine, waddled over to the counter and leaned on it.

"Yes, I wanted to know if you rent tuxedos?"

"Yes, we do. When do you need it?"

"Saturday night."

"We can do that. Let's go and measure."

As they walked toward the back, the young women glanced up from their sewing with envy as the boss preceded the boy with the chiseled face and strong, square jaw.

He left a deposit and promised to return the following day to pick up the pieces he had chosen: one-button peak lapel cutaway jacket, pants, Diamond Royal vest, cummerbund, pique wing collar shirt, black and silver stud and cufflink set, and just for fun, ivory formal tuxedo clip suspenders.

After picking up the tuxedo, he returned home and checked the yellow pages for limousine companies. Several disconnected numbers later, a call rang through. "Chauffeurs on Call."

"I'd like to rent a car and driver for tomorrow night."

"Yes, sir. How many people?"

"Five of us."

"Is it a special occasion? Do you have a theme in mind?"

"No special occasion, just getting together with friends."

"For how long and starting when?"

"Well, how about you pick me up at seven, and then we'll go get the others. Then I want to take a tour around the city especially the lakes and then go to McDonalds."

"McDonalds?"

"Yes. Is something wrong?"

"No, but we usually don't get requests to go to McDonalds. How old did you say you are?"

"I didn't. But I'm nineteen. It's just a special evening."

"Okay. Just between you and me, better you go to McDonalds than a lot of places boys your age might be going. So maybe a couple hours?"

"Yeah, two or three. How much will that be?"

"Our rates are thirty dollars an hour so for three hours it would be ninety dollars. I need a credit card to hold the order."

"Can't I just pay when we are picked up?"

"No we don't do that. We need a credit card for other reasons too e.g. if something is damaged by your group."

"Or if we steal the car?" They both laughed.

"Though I'll admit," said the woman at the rental shop, "you sound like a nice boy. Not one who would trash a car. Maybe you could take my son with you."

"Maybe some day. Okay. Let me get a credit card." He ran to his room and found the credit card his aunt had given him for school and made him swear would only be used for education. He returned and read the number and code to the clerk.

The following night, when five young men walked into McDonalds, one dressed in a tuxedo and the others in street clothes, followed by an older man with a satchel, no one paid them any mind until after the five sat. Minneapolis was full of its quota of strange people. But then, the chauffer, dressed in livery, opened a bag and removed a crisp, white linen tablecloth. He snapped it in the air and by some magic it billowed above the boys and then covered the table perfectly. The boys leaned back in the booth to give him room.

From the bag, the driver pulled out four crystal goblets in molded, plastic cases, removed them one by one and sat one in front of each partygoer. The boys picked up the glasses and pretended to drink, their pinkie fingers extended in the air.

Next, he produced four white, linen napkins rolled around silver cutlery and held with a slim silver ring. These he placed to right of each boy. To their credit, they didn't immediately grab them and unroll the napkin except for one boy who slid the ring off the napkin and onto his finger for a one-finger salute.

Last, mimicking Mary Poppins, the chauffer dug one more time into the black bag and took out four china plates with silver filigree around the edges. After placing a plate in front of each boy, he extracted a white napkin from his pants pocket, unfolded it, and draped it over his left arm. From his jacket pocket he removed a small pad and pen. "May I take your orders, please?"

Like children, the boys giggled and punched each other in the arm. "You go first. No, you."

The waiter stood in perfect silence with perfect posture as if he were at the Ritz waiting on corporate bigwigs until finally he turned to the organizer of the party and broke the logjam with, "Would you like to go first?"

When the waiter returned with the food, he removed each burger from the bag, unwrapped it and using the wrapper, placed it on the china plate. The fries he upended over each plate. Drinks were poured like wine from a bottle into the crystal glasses.

The five ate in splendor amid the Styrofoam cups and plastic ware of the other customers. They talked about sports, bragging a lot, and girls, lying mostly, and their second year of college coming up while children slid down a blue tunnel and climbed up yellow net.

After the meal, the group piled back into the limousine for a tour of the lakes, the campus and the new convention and sports center on the water. They drove to the rich area of town and tried to sneak into the gated communities. Finally, the chauffeur dropped off the guests one by one. At every stop, the boy got out of the car and gave each friend a long hug. When the car reached the final drop off, the boy handed the driver a thirty-dollar tip. "No way. That's much too big a tip for three hours."

"Take it. I don't need it. You were very nice. Thank you."

Inside the house, the boy carefully removed the tuxedo and packed it neatly in its box. On top, he laid the receipt from the rental store. He put the pawnshop receipt next to it on the bed. He dressed in his favorite blue jeans and Save the Whales sweatshirt, white socks and red tennis shoes, picked up the car keys, a blanket and a pillow and went to the garage.

The car door of the old Ford Escort creaked when he opened it. Though it had over two hundred thousand miles on it, it still started in the Northern winters and got him where he was going. Now it would do it again. He started the car and rolled down the front windows.

He didn't think about his mother or what her reaction would be. She had made it clear that now that he was grown, he was on his own, expected to be an adult and a friend, not a scarecrow lurking around like Icabod Crane.

He didn't think about his brother. Jim had told him things would get better if he could just hang on. But life was different for Jim. He was a simple guy. He wanted girls and sports and any kind of job. Jim was like all the other guys, he fit in; he understood them.

He didn't think about his dad who refused to take responsibility for anything as if he were always the helpless victim of a hostile world. If his sons failed to bring him back his long lost sports fame, they were useless.

He did think about his baby sister. Only a half-sister, she had been born when he was eleven, and he lived with his mother then. He had played with the baby like a doll, a beautiful, blond, blue-eyed, talking doll. He carried her everywhere and when she could walk, she tagged behind him, always at his heel making the other boys laugh. She had seemed to know him unlike others, as if they had met before in a parallel universe.

She would miss him. She would care. But he could no longer protect her. Besides, she had strength beyond his. She seemed far older than he in wisdom and understanding. She could fend for herself. He had.

He visualized the shelter he had constructed in the woods in Canada and how the park police had destroyed it. He recalled the vistas he had seen on the Appalachian Trail and when he turned another way, the oozing sore of mountain top removal. He ached for the pike in Warner Lagoon who suffocated because of the growth of reed canary grasses that steal all the oxygen. This tasted like truth.

He curled up on his side across the front seat, spread out the blanket to cover his long frame, wedged the pillow over the padded door handle, closed his eyes and went to sleep.

The Arenas

I.   Playground

The teams were picked today.
Tomorrow it's the old friends,
then the relationships, the heartbreaks, the prom dates,
each group huddled desperately together
beneath their picture frame.
Then all the pictures fade and curl,
glass cracks under the weight of the dust.
They move and the miles swallow up
all memories of belonging.
Everyone packs up, or throws out, or sells off their trophies.
All but one.

II.   Traffic

Years passed with nothing
but the boy's pleas and the parents' refusals
before they opened the door
and a puppy ran into the child's grasp.
A deal of responsibility was struck.
The boy was never happier.
But soon the puppy ate more food,
more attention, more patience, more care
than the boy had ever imagined.
Every day, every walk,

he feared his puppy
would wrestle loose from the leash
and run wild and hopeless
into the long, black road by his side.

III. Dollhouse

Thick, warm grass embraced the house
and sank beneath the kids racing footfalls
as dad pulled into the driveway,
his top down and his eyes alight.
At dinner the conversation played
like a skipping record,
dad may get a promotion,
mom heard new gossip,
the boy watched something on TV
and ever since wouldn't stop begging for a dog.
But the girl just sat and smiled and giggled on cue,
just like all good little girls should,
but her mind never strayed far from the new dollhouse
waiting for her up in her room.
The little dad was just about to pull into the driveway,
and the thick, warm grass would sink
beneath the little kids racing footfalls.

IV. Moving Day

Everything was placed lovingly
into the brown cardboard boxes
that filled the trunk.
A final look through all the rooms
found barren floorboards and walls,

dance floors for dust mites and shy long-silent spirits,
that were so well lived with, yet seemed so unaffected.
It was the fourth final look taken that morning,
everyone scared they'd forget something,
something vital or trivial or anything at all
that, after the car pulled away, would be gone forever.
They carried the last box to the car in silence,
and wept into the rearview mirror.

Workers in Trees

It's a small town. So, when I saw the WORKERS IN TREES sign, I knew there were three men on the local crew. Irv, who grew tomatoes. Stephen Herbert (first and last name always—never just Steve or Stephen). And Raf, whose wife had died of breast cancer, leaving him to raise their two daughters (9 and 12) and one son (7).

I waved as I drove past. Raf and Irv waved back. Stephen Herbert ignored me.

My older sister, Elizabeth, was in the passenger seat and said, "You know these guys?"

"Yeah," I said, "but even if I didn't know them I'd wave—it's local etiquette."

Elizabeth had taken the train out to where I lived, so we could drive together to visit our father. Our mother had been gone for a decade. Long story. Long illness.

I didn't see my father that often. I visited him only when Elizabeth and I went together. She could remember a time when our father had been happier. Frank (my younger brother, who now lived in Tennessee) and I had no such memories. It was as if there were two different families. The one that had started in Italy ("the old country") and had immigrated to the United States when Elizabeth was a few months old, and then another, sour, family after I arrived and then Frank. I had asked Elizabeth, many times, "What changed?" She didn't know.

70

Elizabeth had always gotten along better with our father than I did. She was married, had children, and wore dresses. I was always in jeans. Divorced. No kids.

"I really should track down that gypsy who told me, when I was 23, that I would have four children," I said—it must have seemed a non sequitur to Elizabeth—"and get my dollar back."

The car radio was on, and Elizabeth and I began singing "Addicted to Love." Close harmony. The kind you can do if you're family and your vocal cords are mostly the same DNA.

"Hey," I said. "Remember the time when I wouldn't eat my breakfast, and Dad pushed my face into the cereal bowl?"

"Vaguely," said Elizabeth.

But I remembered. It was Elizabeth who had wiped the milk and tears from my face.

To the left of the highway, a man and a woman were kayaking toward a small bay. It occurred to me that it might never be this wonderful for them again. The calm water. Deep shadows in the trees.

It made me think of Andrew. When I first met him, he had this charming way of pulling at the hair that fell over his forehead. By the time we split up, I was hatching plans of sneaking up on him while he was sleeping and gluing that goddamn hair to his forehead.

Elizabeth was always prepared when visiting our father. Had something planned to pass the hours. She'd called him weeks ago and asked him to create a genealogical chart.

"He drew a family tree," Elizabeth said. "I can't wait to see it. Dad has information from three or four generations back. We have to get him to talk now. There is no later."

After we made the arc into my father's driveway, I turned off the engine, and Elizabeth and I sat in the car for a minute. Not talking. Then Elizabeth said, "Ready?"

We walked into the little yellow house that our father had moved to after he retired. He was in the kitchen, wearing a sleeveless T-shirt. His chest and arms, armored, defined. I kissed my father, dutifully, on the forehead. He stood, impassive, as I performed this filial task. I had no recollection of his ever kissing us.

While Elizabeth issued her version of the official kiss, I looked at the genealogical chart that was spread out on the kitchen table. My father had drawn it as a tree: one big trunk (the family name on it), smaller and smaller branches, and then leaves. My father's drawing skills were primitive; the chart was beautiful.

Poor Elizabeth, I thought.

I waited while Elizabeth helped our father serve us his strong coffee. As soon as Elizabeth was seated, she pulled out her notepad. "Dad, where do you want to start?" she said.

"Your great-great-grandfather was named Antonio," said my father, aiming his thick hand toward the chart. "He was a fisherman and he had four children, Chris, George, John, and Marko. Chris and George also became fishermen, but John became a priest. Marko died when he was still a boy—11 years old."

Elizabeth wrote each name in her book, and fisherman, fisherman, priest.

"What did Marko die of?" she asked.

"He cut his hand and got a fever. There was no doctor," my father said. "Of Antonio's sons, George is your great-grandfather. He had three children. Peter. Constantine. Nicholas."

All the names were on the branches; I could see them from where I sat.

"Peter built boats," my father continued. "Constantine built houses. Nicholas had an olive grove. He argued with the neighbor about property lines. The neighbor said he would sue. Nicholas let him take the land. To go to court was shameful in those days."

Elizabeth had written: boat maker, house builder, olive grove, court, shame. Her handwriting was orderly. Mine had always been a scrawl.

My father moved his attention to the next branch, "You already know that Nicholas was your grandfather . . ."

Elizabeth interrupted. "Wait a second, Dad. These were all the children?"

"Yes," my father lifted his paw for a moment and then placed it back on the chart. "Your grandfather had three children: Thomas, Alex, and me."

"What about Barbara?" said Elizabeth.

Barbara was my father's older sister. She had drowned, in the old country, at the age of 19.

"What about her?"

"You didn't mention her."

"She got married. She didn't carry the family name."

"But I asked you earlier if you had written down all the children."

"I did."

Elizabeth checked her notes, "For instance, my great-great-grandfather Antonio didn't have daughters?"

"Oh," said my father, with a slight toss of his hands. "He had plenty of daughters."

This is what I'd been waiting for—for the elisions in the family tree to register on Elizabeth.

"Dad," said Elizabeth, "do you know any of the daughters' names?"

"No, but one of them married Basil, who lived in another village. Basil kept goats. Her dowry included a small herd of goats."

Elizabeth took a close look at the chart's newest branches. Our father was listed; our mother was not. Elizabeth and I were not on the tree. Nor were Elizabeth's children. But there, written on the leaves, was our brother and his sons.

"I'm following the family name," my father said.

Hours later, back in the car, Elizabeth said, "You weren't surprised."

"Nope. I used up my surprise about Dad a long time ago."

"Where've I been?" Elizabeth said.

"You've been keeping the peace," I said. "That was your job."

"How come you knew?"

"Elizabeth, I always knew. Once—I couldn't have been more than six—I was walking down the street with Dad. That was unusual, just the two of us, walking. I was wearing a red dress, with lace along the top. Dad was holding my hand. That was unusual too. We bumped into a friend of his from the old country. The friend pointed to me and said, 'Yours?' And Dad said yes. And then his friend said, 'How many children do you have?' And Dad said, 'I have one child. And two daughters. I remember thinking that was crazy, because I knew there were three of us."

"Huh," said Elizabeth. It wasn't a word; it was a piece of air pushed out of her.

It wasn't yet dark when we got back to my town. I braked at the stop sign on White Street. On the other side of the intersection, Irv—one of the men from the crew we'd passed that morning—was standing in his garden with his wife, Belinda. They were holding hands.

"Sweet," Elizabeth said when she saw them.

"Maybe," I said.

Elizabeth gave me a look.

"Excuse me," I said. "Just being cynical."

As I neared her house, Belinda flapped her arm in a signal for me to stop and, when I did, poked her friendly face in the window. She and Irv were still holding hands.

"Hi, Anna," said Belinda. "Howyadoin' today?" She didn't wait for me to answer before saying, "Good. Good. Good." I believe that, in that little space before her "Good. Good. Good" I could have said, "I just had my spleen removed, without anesthesia," and Belinda would have just sailed right on to "Good. Good. Good."

"Belinda, this is my sister, Elizabeth."

"Nice to meet you." Belinda stuck her non-Irv hand toward Elizabeth.

"And Elizabeth, this is Irv," I said to Irv's hand.

"Irv, let's give Anna some of your tomatoes," Belinda said. She turned to me, "You know that Irv grows the most wonderful tomatoes."

"Great tomatoes," I said. It was true.

"Where are the paper bags?" said Irv.

"On the garden chair."

Irv and Belinda had the kind of marriage where you start off with two people and you end up with less than one. I'd been listening to them ever since I moved to town: "Irv, where are my gloves?" "Belinda, what's the phone number for the hardware store?"

"Did you have a nice drive?" Belinda asked.

"Yes," said Elizabeth.

Belinda wagged her head. "Glad to hear it. Live in the moment," she said and then turned toward Irv.

"Irv, where are those tomatoes?"

"I'm getting them," said Irv.

"I swear, he gets so easily distracted," said Belinda. "I should get one of those Burberry computers. That way I could keep track of him."

Irv appeared with the tomatoes. I thanked his hand.

When Elizabeth and I got to my house, I promptly banged my own hand, hard, on the edge of the desk. "Live in the moment," I said, hopping around and agitating my hand. "I'd like to live in the moment. But not this one. I'd like to select one from 10 years ago. February. A Wednesday. 3:24 p.m. That was an excellent moment. I want to live in that one."

Elizabeth went to bed right after dinner. I wasn't sleepy. I sat in the armchair and looked out the window. I could see the glow of the town's one lamppost several blocks away. I stepped outside, stood in the still air, and then got into the car. I rode around, no place in particular. Main Street. The gas station. Sammy's Pancake Shoppe. The side streets.

When I got to the street where Raf lived with his three motherless children, I parked at the corner. Raf's house was in the middle of the block. One downstairs window was lit.

That night I dreamt I was ringing the doorbell of the apartment that Andrew and I had shared in the city. In the morning, when I woke up, the ceiling seemed too close. I needed to get out. A hike would do me good.

I ran some errands and, late in the afternoon, dragged out my bicycle and headed toward Taft Mountain. By the time I reached Plank Road it had begun to rain. I got to the trailhead later than I had expected. If I started up now, I'd be coming down in the dark. But under a full moon. After college, I'd spent three drifting years in a cabin in Colorado. It was there that I'd once heard the spine-straightening whine of a cougar. There, too, that I'd learned to be comfortable in the mountains. I'd been up Taft many times. It was a pipsqueak compared to the Rockies. I grabbed the flashlight I kept in my bicycle bag and started up the trail. The rain had stopped, but the woods were juicy. Partway up, I veered off trail to visit a pond that I knew was there. I watched a dragonfly—blue and gold spots—helicopter over the water and then I returned to the trail and kept climbing. At the top of Taft Mountain, the sky was floating. Far away. Blue-gray. Everything paused. Something, not quite mist, was rising up like a vague memory. Twilight.

When I'd lived in the Rockies, I would stand outside in the evening and try to perceive the moment when twilight turned to night. I never managed to find that seam. I'd be saying, it's twilight, it's twilight. And then I'd realize that it was night. But I hadn't seen it turn over, hadn't caught one thing becoming the other. The same happened now. It was twilight. Then it was night. I'd missed the change. The moon was a fuzz, the color of a moth's wing.

* * *

Every once in a while I bumped into Stephen Herbert at the post office. This time he said, "You'd best cut down some of those trees in your front yard."

"Hello, Stephen Herbert," I said.

"You'd best cut down those trees." He was standing too close to me. He was a large man.

"Why is that?"

"The beeches don't look healthy. A heavy storm could bring one of them down on your roof. Do they creak in the wind?"

"Not that I've noticed."

"It's a good idea to notice." And he walked out the door.

So I called Raf and asked him to take a look at the trees that Stephen Herbert had warned of.

"They're OK," said Raf. "But you need to clear that away." He pointed to where a bulk of a neighbor's tree had split off and lodged in a bifurcation in one of my beeches. It swayed a bit, aiming downward. "That's what's called a widow maker," said Raf. "It's time-consuming work. But I can get you firewood out of it."

"How're your kids?" I asked.

"You always ask that," Raf said. "Thanks. I usually tell you some funny story about how they are. Those stories are true, but it's also true that I don't always know how they are. I hope they're OK. But, since their mother died, who knows?"

"Do they talk about her?"

"Sure. But less now. I don't know when to talk about her, either. You never met Irene."

"No."

"She wanted to die at home," Raf said, his face now in profile. "On the day—right before she died—the kids were at school. She asked to be outside, on the ground. 'That'll make it easier,' she said. So I carried her into the yard. She was on her back, looking at the sky. I was sitting next to her, touching her hand. And that was it. Oh, my god, she looked so beautiful right then. That I remember. But I can't talk about it to my kids. Right?"

"Someday."

"Anyway," said Raf. "What makes you think these trees are a problem?"

"Stephen Herbert said they might come down in a storm."

"Stephen Herbert," said Raf. "I wish I had half his energy. But sometimes I wonder if he isn't like the arsonist who joins the volunteer firefighters. Last week he chain sawed a grove on his own land. The only thing that could have made it look worse was if his property was strewn with the bodies of dead civilians. Do you want these trees cut?"

"Not if they can stay."

"I'd rather not cut a tree, if it can be avoided. To my thinking, it makes a sort of wound. It's your decision, but if you cleared these trees, I would consider it random cutting. Just because something can be done doesn't mean it should be done."

"And vice versa," I said. It always seemed to be a problem for me. What to do. What not to do. What to remove. What to leave in place.

"That sounds enough like wisdom to me," Raf said. "If you want, I'll take care of that widow maker tomorrow. It'll be done by the time you get back from work."

"Agreed," I said. "Let me find my checkbook."

"Pay me after I finish. You can drop a check off at my house tomorrow."

"I might be late getting home."

"That's fine," he said.

The next night, I didn't get to Raf's house until 10 p.m. His kids were asleep. We stood in the kitchen. I handed Raf the check.

"Thanks," he said. "Cup of coffee or tea?"

"Tea."

I followed Raf as he headed for a cabinet. He turned around suddenly and bumped into me.

"I'm sorry," he said. "I didn't see you standing there."

"That's probably because I wasn't entirely there."

He laughed. He was a silent laugher. "Good one," he said.

"OK, here's the usual question. How are your kids?"

"Kathy, the twelve year old, has decided to cheerlead for world peace."

"What does that mean?"

"I don't know yet. And Lynn plays a lot of soccer. She'll get strong legs. Good for standing on. And Harry—he just turned seven—oh, that reminds me."

Raf walked toward the front door. Coats, rain boots, hats and caps, kids' things were piled on a bench. He unzipped one of the knapsacks.

"Like I was saying, Harry just turned seven and announced that he wanted a Barbie for his birthday. I asked if he meant a Ken doll. No, he meant Barbie. That surprised me. He's so much a boy kind of boy, if you know what I mean. But I figured what do I know and I bought him Barbie. I haven't seen that Barbie since. I'm curious."

Raf reached into the knapsack and extracted a coloring book, three sticks of partially unwrapped gum, a crushed crayon box. And then Barbie. Harry had taken an automatic weapon from some action figure and had transferred that firepower to Barbie.

"There's Barbie," I said.

"Yeah," said Raf, "and she's packin' that's for sure."

Raf shrugged, put Barbie back, and zipped up the knapsack.

"Let's have that tea," he said.

We did, until the phone rang. Raf leapt for it so it wouldn't wake the kids.

"Hello," he said.

There was a long pause, while whoever was on the other end of the line talked.

"Anything else?" said Raf

Long pause.

"Then what?" said Raf. His voice was neutral.

Long pause.

"That all?" said Raf.

Long pause.

"More?" said Raf.

The voice on the other end of the line began to sound agitated. Raf pulled his ear away from the receiver, to avoid the smack of the caller's banging the phone down.

"Problem?" I said.

"Obscene phone call. Sounded like a teenage boy. I figured if I gave him enough time, he'd run out of things to say."

"Did he?"

"I think so. Because the last thing he said was, 'Don't ever call me again.'"

It was my turn to laugh. "Good one," I said.

* * *

The original plan had been that Elizabeth and I would visit our father together, as usual. But she had to drive her mother-in-law to an emergency doctor's appointment.

"Let's postpone the visit," I said.

"Can't. There are forms that need to be filled out for Dad's medical insurance," said Elizabeth. "As usual, we've left it for the last minute. Dad can't fill them out by himself. One of us has to—actually, you have to—go. Tomorrow. Sorry."

To make matters worse, my car was in the shop. Yesterday, Belinda, who kept track of every vehicle in town, had left a message on my answering machine, asking if I needed a lift anywhere. Reluctantly, I called her and requested a ride to the bus that would take me into the city. From there, I could get another bus to my father's house.

"How's tennis?" I said, once I was in Belinda's car. I knew she liked to play.

"Not good because Patty—you know Patty, my doubles partner—can't play for six weeks. She was going back for a lob and fell and tore her ACLU in her knee."

I had no idea who Patty was and I was surprised to learn that she kept the ACLU in her knee.

"Irv had that once," said Belinda. "But it wasn't as bad as his heart attack."

"I didn't know Irv had a heart attack."

"Four years ago. Poor Irv. They had to do that test to figure out just how clogged his blood vessels were. I kept asking, 'How is he?' and the doctors kept saying, 'We'll know more after we do the castration.'"

"Catheterization?"

"Yes. And wouldn't you know it, Irv had his heart attack the same time I was taking care of my mother. She had that Old Timers disease."

"Alzheimer's?"

"Yes. Old Timers."

Two bus rides later, and my father was waiting for me at the station. I got into his car; we drove to his house. After lunch, I filled out the medical forms. Then he said, "I want to show you something."

I followed him into the tiny room that adjoined the kitchen. There was a new Army cot covered with a gray blanket. A wooden chair next to it. The only other thing in the room was a freestanding metal closet. Or locker. It was bigger than a locker and smaller than a closet.

"This will be your room," my father said.

What was he talking about? I never stayed over.

"You'll move here and take care of me. I'm getting old."

Alzheimer's? Old Timers? I looked at my father. He was serious.

"I can't do that, Dad?" It had been crazy to come here without Elizabeth.

"Why not?"

"Because I'm 39 years old and I have a job, a life."

My father's look was the same stony cloud I had known when I was a child. The mirror that reflected nothing. The cave. He was angry. Sputtering. Sounds unlinked to words. I thought he might have a heart attack. Right here. Right now. I would have to call 911.

But he found his words.

"You have a life?"

"Yes, I have a life."

"Your life is nothing."

So here we were. This, in my father's mind was the sum of my years. The truth. The cot. The locker.

I walked to the kitchen, took my jacket from where it hung on the back of a chair.

Where are you going?" His voice was exploding. I looked at the side of his face, at the scar remaining from where acid had burned him in a factory accident.

"I'm going home," I said, knowing all the while that I barely had one. The house, empty without Andrew, but still—something. With a real bed in it. And a closet, and a blanket that wasn't gray. Not much. But not this.

My father followed me into the kitchen, his hands in fists. What if he tried to stop me? We were on opposite sides of the table. Something inside me said, move fast. I slid sideways out the door and toward the road. It would be a couple-of-miles walk to the bus station.

I knew that my father's anger was nothing to trifle with. I hugged the side of the road that edged a marsh. Five or six minutes later, I heard the engine sound and I slipped into the cattails. My father's car sped by, its tires scrambling gravel. I crouched there for an hour, by my watch, until the car passed again, this time going the other way.

I had missed one bus, but the next one finally arrived. It was different from the one that had brought me. The windows on this bus were covered with a scrim, a kind of bus burka. I asked the driver, "How can you see through that?"

"Just fine," he said.

That couldn't be true. Looking out the side window was like looking at the world through a waffle. People who'd come to send off friends and family couldn't see into the bus. As we pulled away, they waved in some theoretical farewell gesture.

*** *** ***

A few days later, it was Raf on the phone. "Anna. I'm calling because I need help with something."

"Sure. What?"

"I have some deer netting stored in the backyard, and somehow— I don't know how—a couple of black rat snakes have gotten twisted in it. Or they were born in a nest there and, as they grew, they grew into the netting. I've got to cut them out of there, but I can't do it alone."

"OK. When?"

I'd said that too quickly. Not exactly a phobia. But there was that one time in Colorado when I'd found myself in uncomfortable proximity to a sleeping rattlesnake. I didn't know how close I wanted to get, voluntarily, to any black rat snakes. They were big. I'd seen them in trees.

"Can you come over now?" said Raf. "The netting is cutting into their skin."

When I got there, Raf was already on the porch. He was armed with garden shears, wire clippers, and a knife.

"Basically," he said, "I need you to hold the netting. Just so you know, black rat snakes aren't venomous. They eat small rodents, birds, bird eggs. But they'll be pretty passive as long as we both stay relaxed. Can you do that?"

"Yes," I said. I had no idea if I could do it.

The rolls of deer netting, some partially opened, rested against an apple tree. A jumble of wire held the rolls together, but chaotically.

There were two snakes, enmeshed, barely capable of motion in any direction. They looked inextricable. There was blood on their scales.

Raf. He stepped into the convoluted puzzle, gently tilted one of the rolls toward me. "Hold this steady," he said.

Starting near the snake's head, Raf snipped away at the netting. I had my back against the apple tree and I was holding wrapped-up fencing. So far, I was doing OK. Until Raf's efforts started working. Slowly, as it was freed, the first snake became mobile and aimed its body away from the netting and toward me. The first thing I felt was its muscle clenching my wrist, a motion that made me suck my breath in. Hello, Freud? I thought, as if on a phone call to the—what was he? Austrian?—father of psychiatry. Here I am with a couple of snakes and a guy named Raf who is . . . who is? I don't know exactly who. What's your opinion on this imagery, Siggy?

Raf, quiet and concentrating, cut away another section of netting, allowing the snake to continue its peristaltic journey, now up onto my forearm. I remembered reading, somewhere, that black rat snakes were excellent climbers. A small nausea hit me. The snake's scales were dry, and not (as I had imagined) smooth. Instead, they had small ridges that grabbed the skin of my arm each time the snake was able to inch upward. The snake was shiny black. Sprinkles of white color appeared between its scales as it shifted. I stood as still as I could. Sweat streaked down my forehead. I could now see the snake's chin, where white markings began and seemed to extend down its underbody. Raf said these kinds of snakes had no venom. But all snakes can bite, right?

Raf was doing his best to keep the snake's head away from me, but he still had to work at the next place that was reachable.

Whenever it could, the snake continued its deliberate flow and it was now at my shoulder. It curled, and its unblinking eye was next to mine. Its tail end, easily eight feet away, remained wedged in the netting.

This was all taking a long time.

"How are you doing?" said Raf.

I didn't answer. He glanced at me. I closed my eyes, to signal I don't know what.

"I have to leave this snake partly free and start on the next one," said Raf. "They're entwined. I can't get this one out until I get the damn wire off the second one."

Freeing the second snake turned out to be a quicker job. It was up near my chest before I felt ready. My heart jumped.

As soon as Raf extracted its tail from the netting, the second snake slithered, slithered—onomatopoeia, I thought—and it was gone, up the tree, and gone.

"Looks like that one is going to be fine," said Raf.

But the first snake was still trapped, most of its length caught in the netting. Painstakingly, one coil at a time, Raf freed it. With each increase in mobility, the snake took another rotation around me. It constricted around my waist in a calligraphic pattern.

My emotional stamina was fading. Raf had said to hold steady. Nothing, I thought, is as steady as a dead person. I should own up. I was dead. With a snake spiraling around me. Whoever I was before—the person married to Andrew—was dead. Lots of people die before they die. Like the ones in comas. Dead, sort of. Alive, sort of. Maybe I'd feel better if I gave up, or if I decided I was someone I didn't know. Newness might not be so hard. It might be like a little bump on a suburban road, signifying that I had passed over into something new and strange. Something new and strange, wasn't that Shakespeare? A Midsummer Night's Dream? No. The Tempest. Ariel singing. What came next? Da-dum, da-dum, da-dum. Something, something, something, sea change. Or did the sea change part come before new and strange? Oh, I've got it.

"Full fathom five thy father lies;

Of his bones are coral made;

Those are pearls that were his eyes:

Nothing of him that doth fade

But doth suffer a sea-change

Into something rich and strange."

The half-free snake curled up from my waist and shoulder, its head near mine, and flicked its tongue. The tongue was blue and, as advertised, forked. Another minute and the snake had most of its body to work with. It turned into a kind of Möbius strip, spinning, in place, around itself. A sequential loosening of its corkscrewed body from around my body, and the snake slipped up the tree.

I sat down and bowed my head. Raf sat next to me.

"Want to wash off in the pool?" he said.

I nodded, took off my sneakers, walked into the water with all my clothes on, and swam. Lap after lap. My brain kept saying, "Don't come out until you're new. Don't come out until you're new." It was, I discovered, possible to weep underwater.

From the pool, I could see Raf's kids heading down the street toward home. Kathy, dressed in her cheerleader uniform, was walking their family dog. A bulldog named Bicep. Lynn was escorting a soccer ball along the sidewalk. She handled it like it was her best friend. Harry lagged behind, bent over, peering at the sidewalk. His knapsack was as big as his torso. Barbie was in that knapsack, with her Uzi.

After the children entered the house, I climbed from the water. My clothes clung to me.

"Could I apply to management for a towel?" I said.

"Absolutely," said Raf. "Come on in."

I stepped inside the back door. Harry was belly down on the carpet, reading a comic. Raf's daughters were watching ballet on television. The ballerinas were in tutus.

"Hi, Anna," said Kathy.

"Hi, Kathy. Hi, Lynn. Hi, Harry," I said. I felt soggy.

"Dad, see the costumes on these ballerinas," Kathy said. "They're like pastries."

"Or sachets," said Raf.

Kathy and Lynn rolled over one another, giggling.

"Dad," said Harry. "I'm hungry. What's for lunch?"

"I've got to get going," I said.

"No," said Raf. He was holding a towel. "Stay. Will you stay for lunch?"

I'd been embraced by two rat snakes and now I felt like a wet rat. A word was clanging around in my brain. The word was almost. My life was a string of almosts. There was the Ph.D. that I'd done all the work on, except for finishing the thesis. The consulting business that Elizabeth and I had started but sold—when Elizabeth got married and I didn't think I could keep it going on my own. And there was my marriage to Andrew. We almost made it though, Andrew and I. Almost.

Here I was, standing just inside Raf's back door. In the? Entryway? Or is that just for the space near the front door? Antechamber? Too fancy. Foyer? Not exactly. I was in one of those twilight spaces again. The kind of space I'd always lived in. Not a home, but almost.

And here was Raf, repeating his question. "Will you stay for lunch?"

Guitar

Driving home at 1.00am on Kelvin Grove Road.

The red car in front,

irrational, refuses the corner

hits the telegraph pole

in a flower of light.

There is no other traffic.

I stop and run back to the hissing machine.

I can see the driver is a girl with dark hair.

Her shape is all wrong.

A guitar protrudes its head from the windscreen.

A man in shorts comes out of the nearest house.

'I've rung the ambulance' he says,

lifts one bare foot, then the other.

'Her neck is broken', I tell him.

I'm not sure how I know this,

where these words come from,

or why, when he returns in slippers,

I drive away.

White Noise

They were doing a dollar dance. Chase thought it was a stupid idea for a bunch of teenagers, but every guy there was waving bills at the birthday girl. They whirled her around the room, tucking money into her hand or pocket before passing her to the next set of arms. Her smile seemed a little too wide and fixed, shoulders stiff, but she let herself be passed from person to person. She kept her chin tucked down toward her chest, hiding the recent injury, and pretended that she wasn't intimidated by being in a room full of people who could still talk. She was doing a good job, too.

She landed in her good friend Dekker's embrace, and relaxed against him. Chase clenched his fists as he watched him bend over and whisper in Adrian's ear. She lifted her chin for the first time, exposing the barest hint of scarring above her high-necked shirt, and smiled in relief. Adrian's arms were wrapped around Dekker's neck, and she grinned over his shoulder. A few seconds of swaying back and forth, a twenty dollar bill tucked into a back pocket, and three twirls later, they were almost directly in front of Chase. He sidestepped behind a guy from school, and stayed long enough to see the confusion cross her face as she spun into someone else's arms.

His skin itched with the irrational urge to pound the guy pressed up against her. Instead Chase slammed out of the house, almost knocking over the gift table where his tiny red package balanced on top, and pounded down the stairs. Dekker caught up with him there, spinning him around with a hand on his shoulder.

"Don't Chase."

"What, dude?" he asked, shrugging the hand off, and stepping away.

"Don't 'what' me. I saw that, even if she didn't."

Light, flickering and full of movement, poured out of the windows behind them, illuminating the wrap around porch and azalea bushes. Chase swatted a bloom, scattering soft pink petals across the walkway, and looked at Dekker in icy silence.

"Your mood swings are getting old. Get a grip on your tantrum, and go the hell back inside."

"Screw you, man," Chase said and walked across the yard.

"You even care that she's gonna be looking for you?" Dekker yelled behind him.

Chase kept going, ignoring Dekker's last insult of "asshole coward!" and a few other choice words about getting the hell over whatever was bothering him until he neared the woods that edged the property. He glanced back at the house occasionally, at the one and a half story cabin he'd practically grown up in, as he headed to the darkness of an old, favorite tree. The wet, heavy atmosphere smothered everything, even the deep thrum of base from the party. The big trees that ringed the yard, oak, maple and magnolia, helped swallow up sound until it was just Chase and a chorus of crickets. It made Georgia nights perfect for silence and solitude.

Crouching to avoid low hanging limbs, he moved to the trunk and began to climb. He snaked his body between thin, tightly packed branches, big waxy leaves and lemon scented blossoms brushing his face on the way up. He stopped a few limbs up, sprawled vertically across a succession of branches. A narrow bough cradled his hips from behind, his feet lightly rested below, and his forearms were propped above for balance. The house was visible through the foliage, and he watched shadows gyrate and sway in front of the windows to music he could no longer hear. In the dark to his left, he saw the dim, far-off glow of his own porch light. Rolling his neck back and forth to ease tension, he closed his eyes. It was so much easier to be out in the warm, dark night than to be in at that party where he felt like a stranger among his friends.

Light and sound cascaded into the night as someone stepped onto the front porch and closed the door. The person was no more than a shadow backlit by the amber glow pouring from the windows, but he knew who it was. No one else stood like that, all hunched in on themselves like if they drew in tight enough they could just disappear. She should have been inside enjoying her eighteenth birthday party, the final hurrah before graduation. Instead Adrian was peering around the corners of the house, and looking in the cars parked in the driveway. Searching for him.

Chase watched for a while as her silhouette wandered farther from the house. Stopping near the tree, bleached in shades of grey by the moonlight, she tilted her head back and looked up at the stars. They sparkled this far from town, layer upon layer of light in the endlessly deep night sky. She would have been pretty if it wasn't for the scarring across her neck, a thick, surgically precise white line across her throat and the lumpy irregular circle just above her collar bone. The scars were glowing with an unsettling brightness in the stark light, and made it impossible for Chase to admire the long shock of hair that reached down to slim hips or the freckle sprinkled pert nose he used to tweak. Yes, without the scars, she was perfectly pretty.

Just seeing the scars was enough to make his clammy skin prick with heat. It stabbed along his arms, and up around his tightening neck muscles. Around him, leaves began to rustle slightly, stirring up the sweet lemon scent of the magnolia blossoms. The limbs trembled, then began to shake as Chase closed his hands around a slim bough and squeezed. The skin across his knuckles stretched painfully as he took two long, deep breaths. Those scars, innocently white in the moonlight, haunted him, and he could barely control his adverse reaction. She really was almost beautiful.

As Adrian wandered closer, sweat slipped off his brow and ran into the corner of his eye, pooling with the moisture that was already there. Air shuddered out of lungs that were suddenly too tight for comfort as Chase fought to control his emotions, a warring of gut twisting anguish, deep seated revulsion the sight of those scars brought on, and something else. That unidentifiable thing, like a string behind his belly button pulling him toward her, that was the hardest to fight, the hardest to understand. The tree rustled below, and he imagined her pressing her face into a big, silky blossom, brushing fingers over big, waxy leaves, smiling. She loved this big, old tree as much as he did. Pulling his trembling hands away from the branch, Chase sucked in a slow, deep breath and held it, silently willing her to go away.

One minute passed, then two. Adrian was no longer visible through the gap in the limbs. All he could see was tall stalks of grass bleached to bone and the distant two-story cabin, doll-house small and jeweled with light. The silence wasn't comforting with someone else wandering around in it, but was rather sinister, like he was being hunted. There was another muted rustle then something soft brushed Chase's ankle. It promptly clamped on and jerked.

Without his hands up for balance, Chase's body slithered off his perch. His head rocked backward, bouncing off the branch that had cradled his hips, and the back of his knees hooked around a different limb. He swung upside down and around, crashing through the lower limbs to hit the ground on his forearms and stomach. The fall wasn't far, but he had enough momentum to make it hurt like hell. One leg was still lifted off the ground slightly, pulled up and back by shoelaces tangled in a cluster of magnolia blossoms. Dirt and debris clung to damp skin, uncomfortable and gritty. Wheezing for breath, he rolled clear of the limbs and flopped on his back.

Adrian was standing a few feet away, hand on her hip. She tilted her head to one side and stared at him. She was smiling, but it was both amused and cruel, a look only the very oldest of friends can give. Bugs fluttered all around, black specks against the ghostly pale backdrop. He laid there, shoelaces still trapped by a thick tangle of leaves, breathing in the crisp, heady scent of crushed blooms.

"What the hell, Adrian," he groaned.

She didn't answer. She couldn't. The stupid car wreck had taken that ability forever. She spread her feet and crossed her arms, looming over him. Chase gritted his teeth in frustration, tried to pull his foot free. There was no point in arguing with a cripple who couldn't yell back. He smacked his palms down in the bare, hard packed dirt he'd landed in and pushed up, aggravated almost beyond endurance.

"Just go the fuck back inside, would you?"

Her sneaker landed right on his hip bone, striking a sharper pain than any of the limbs he'd collided with. All the hurt and confusion disappeared, solidified into an all-consuming fury that pulsed through him like a live thing. Lashing out, he slapped a leg out from under her hard. He saw a flash of wide, startled eyes as she toppled down on him. Rolling in a tangle of knees and elbows, their weight pulled his shoe free and sent broken twigs and pieces of leaves flying. The night was still hot and heavy, and even Chase's furious grunts and the thwack of fist meeting flesh were muffled into near silence.

A lifetime of wrestling together made them pretty even adversaries, but after a particularly sharp punch to the ear, Chase used his size and weight to pin Adrian down. He'd gotten bigger than her a long, long time ago. He wrapped his legs around hers and pulled them out straight so she had no leverage, flattening her to the ground with his chest and hips. One of her hands was pinned between them, thumb resting against his collarbone. The grit of sweat and dirt was more noticeable there, where skin touched skin.

Holding her wrist above her head, Chase levered himself up with his free arm just enough to look at her. Both of them were panting for breath, their chests pressing tight then easing apart. She didn't struggle against him, just laid there and glared. A strand of hair was pasted to one cheek, an inky swirl across dove grey. The moon was full and bright, illuminating the crease between her brows, the smudge of dirt across her temple, the way her top lip was tucked over the bottom in a pout.

"Well, wasn't that nice? Been a while since I kicked your ass," he said, and she quirked an eyebrow at him, still giving him a dirty look. He was trembling slightly, raging inside with a swirl of black emotion, but his voice was cold and calm, betraying nothing. He put his face close to hers, and said, "Maybe you didn't get it, but I came out here to get away from you."

Why? He saw the question in the moonlight, but it was as silent like they were in an old black and white film. Just facial expression and gesture, and sad, pouty lips to say it all. No sound from her, never again.

"Seriously?" he said. "Four, maybe five weeks out of the hospital, and you're hanging all over every guy in town?"

Honest shock was written across her face. She blinked up at him. Once. Twice. Then she closed her eyes, and shook her head softly. The motion knocked up a tiny cloud of dust and dandelion dander, and Chase let go of her wrist to wave it away.

You're jealous, she mouthed incredulously, lifting her head a little to stare into his eyes. Chase turned his head slightly and gazed out over the yard to avoid the truth of her words. Her body softened under his, no longer straining, and he was suddenly aware of the bare legs pressed against his blue jeans.

"Yeah, right." He eased backward until he was kneeling over her legs. "Nothing to be jealous of. You can't even talk anymore."

He barely twitched out of the way as she jerked her thigh up between his legs. The movement startled him, and he toppled over sideways. Adrian hadn't tried to kick him there since they were eight and he had thrown a football through her 3-D puzzle of Tara from *Gone with the Wind*. She followed him up as he rolled away, and crouched in front of him. The way her nostrils flared told him she was furious, far madder than when she'd knocked him out of the tree, or punched him.

"We are talking now." She mouthed the words slowly, pausing between each word. She used her hands, too, in slow stilting jerks, trying to talk in the way they were teaching her at therapy. Black crescents fringed in pale grey lashes glared at him from inches away as she leaned in so close their noses were almost touching. He was looking right in her eyes like he'd imagined a million times, but he couldn't help but glance down at the scars.

"No we're not," he yelled in her face. "We're not talking. You can't. Don't you get it, you're fucking broken!"

She just stared at him in silence, a little shocked and kind of devastated, and suddenly it was too much. He'd come out searching for some peace, hoping the still dark night would settle over him, and make his head and his heart quiet for the first time since he thought his best friend was going to die in that damn car crash. Instead, he was suffocating. The silence was so loud it roared in his ears like white noise, became static in his thoughts. The landscape was washed in death colors, grey and black, shades of charcoal. The night was like a dead thing, and in a way, so was she.

"You're in there dancing, like there's nothing wrong. But, there is." He knew it was unfair, remembered the way she'd tucked her chin over her scars, but he couldn't stop. The words poured out with perfect clarity. She was easing away from him now, lowering her chin again. She wrapped her arms around herself, slumping into her newly acquired, self-conscious posture.

"They all feel the same way, you know? Came to see the poor little crippled girl. That's why all those guys were smiling at you. Pity." He raised his voice again, the rich huskiness cracking with all the frustration he felt. "Nobody can look at you. Not without seeing those," he said gesturing to her neck.

Not fair, she mouthed, shaking her head. She stumbled to her feet, and began backing away. Her narrowed eyes and pursed lips radiated defiance; she was almost as angry and upset as he was. But her body was crumpling in on itself slowly, shoulders starting to sag as she moved away.

"Fair?" Chase's laugh was an ugly thing, too hard and clipped for his whiskey smooth voice. He kept ranting, telling her how much it pissed him off that she couldn't be fixed, and he didn't want things to be different. That she shouldn't have smiled or danced with all those boys, it wasn't fair when she should've smiled just for him.

She stood in the high grass, gazing across the yard toward the house where shadows were still flickering across the windows and no one had noticed the birthday girl was missing. She seemed to grow smaller with each word, like she was starting to think maybe he was right. She crouched down to sit, then stood again. She was fidgeting, drifting back toward the house one small step at a time, unsure how to respond.

"How am I supposed to deal, huh? We can't even argue anymore!" he finished, kicking up a chunk of dirt and grass. Something sharp nicked his forehead, and he slapped a hand to it, feeling the sticky ooze of blood and sweat and grit. Breathing loudly, every muscle in his body hard and tight, coiled with tension, he stared open mouthed. Adrian juggled a rock in her left hand, the right empty from the missile she'd just thrown. She might have been crying, but with the moonlight behind her, it was hard to tell. She lifted a finger and pointed, not toward the house, but down the driveway. Away from her, and the party, and all their friends.

Chase stomped away, avoiding the house, and then started jogging down the driveway. He swung at the mailbox as he passed it, the skin of his knuckles bursting under the impact. His eyes itched and stung, and he swiped at them with a bloody hand. Feet pounding against the pavement, he ran hard to get away from what he'd just said to Adrian. His thoughts pulsed through his head in time with his footsteps, broken, broken, broken. His favorite girl in the whole world was broken.

He flew through the dark until he came to the fork in the road that would take him home. The street was lightless, hedged in by dense trees on both sides that formed a canopy. It was blessedly shady on hot summer days, but infinitely black at night. Chase wouldn't have found his way back if his feet hadn't walked the route to Adrian's thousands of times. He went back slowly, again basking in the silence and darkness of the hot summer night. A slight breeze blew up the road, ruffling through the tree-lined tunnel, cooling his skin and his temper.

Everything was twisted up inside him, the unrelenting anger, the aching and tingling where Adrian had touched him, the overwhelming confusion. It was all there, always, just under the surface, a boiling pot of suffering. He just didn't know what to do with it. He scuffed his feet, and dawdled as he came back to the driveway, stopping to straighten the mailbox and pat out the dent in the flimsy tin.

He headed up the driveway, weaving through the cars parked there, wondering if he should go back in, and say something or just wait outside until everybody left. He was a filthy mess after all. As he passed his car, the question was answered. A tiny red package was sitting on the hood, wrapped up a thick, satiny ribbon that sparkled with facets of gold and copper in the faint light from the porch. Chase was close enough to hear the music again, and see the silhouettes swaying behind the curtains to a sweet, slow song. But, he was alone outside with the tiny gift he'd brought for Adrian.

He leaned against the door of his old nova, the metal cool and smooth, and just stared. He was going to give it to her, the tiny, pretty little package, on the night of the accident. It was the thing that should have tipped the scales from friend to lover, and sent them down a whole other path. Then she'd gotten hurt, and he'd gotten angry and their whole world had spun out of control until it was defined by this. A gift, sitting abandoned in the dark. The stinging returned, and tears tracked through the grime on his face because this felt like good-bye.

Anti-Ode for the Boss

Every idea belongs in the trophy case
every decision could stop an earthquake
even the pattern in his tie holds the secret
location to the beginning of civilization
but I won't distract you with the details
of a man who holds an inventory gun
like Wyatt Earp at the O.K Corral,
because *this is not your living room,*
this is the real world honey, darling,
and he's got no time for your kid's pneumonia
the husband that disappeared with your car.
The tightness of his ship could mangle a swarm of nuns,
so be sure to keep your eyes on your own paper,
don't point out the hour he's late, the typos
he pours out like the schnapps in his coffee mug,
even the misspelling of his name is just a quirk.
This is his mark in life: the stool an inch higher
than the rest of the drunks in the bar,
the con with an extra ration of canned beef,
the bum who's too good to give blood.

Another Round of Bullshit Enters a Crowded Room and Won't Stop Talking

Let's play Truth or Dare. I have never been very good with names but you should play along, anyway, because I am so very desperate to answer your questions. I will answer honestly, but only when you're looking me in the eyes. My teeth are pearly white with the residue of my purest intentions and my nails have been polished to hide all the shit that lies beneath them. I promise not to tell you any of this.

Maybe next year will offer a good season for reason. The only luck I've found so far was buried deep beneath a dead oak tree, but then I've always thought hunting to be stupid. I will apply antiseptic to the scratches on my arms before I start blaming you for taking us so far off this conversation's path, and you, you will chug that chalky liquid until I am able to diagnose all the causes of your heart ache. The bruising on your wrists will fade over time, I imagine. And I imagine you a lot. I will blow my smoke in your face and you won't bat an eyelash. I will hand you drinks that you will chug down without asking what's in it. It was imperative that I got here before anywhere else and you are very lucky I have arrived so quickly and in such dizzying speeds, my fantastic prowess trailing behind me and, no, no, I didn't hear what you were saying but don't bother repeating it.

I apologize, I am barely passing for polite around this time every day and you're overrunning any levels of tolerance I'd stored away and really, you should just pass me over for the attention of someone else, someone much more understanding and interesting than I can be, even when I'm here right now in front of you, radiating at my best.

I don't mind, not at all, not from the likes of you, not in the very least.

On Watching Jack Play Guitar

It's romantic to pretend

that bodies are engineered for retention.

As if evolution decided, through

cost-benefit analysis, that the hurt

and rage of living was worth remembering.

Humanity built skin*walls* to fit numbers

and words and times. We were the fittest,

we survived.

We made memory holders, we made

bodies… opened our brains

to foster-home moments, allowing wayward

recollections safe passage. And this life

is worth the regret; the blood in the honey.

Jack proved it. Watching him straighten

his concave confidence and sprout wings

validated the venom of humanity.

Forget harmonic convergence,

he bounded octaves to ascension.

Housekeeping

Every winter Kate collects the hair trapped in her boar bristle brush and saves it in a plastic sandwich bag. The long strands are more white and gray than auburn now. In April she wraps the tresses loosely around pine boughs and maple twigs then sits silent for hours in her blue Adirondack chair in the back yard and watches hummingbirds and chipping sparrows pull hanks of it to line their nests. If she is motionless enough, and silent enough, for long enough, one bird, or maybe two will land on her head and pluck at the source. In autumn when the leaves drop and the cold winds begin to shriek in from the north, she collects the blown down nests and lines her windowsills and coffee tables with them. Her favorite is an oriole pouch, still attached to a branch. Only white curls are threaded through it.

Lucky Carol

Carol has a wooden bowl of two pronged bones knotted together with fine silk thread. Thirty years of unused best poultry wishes with all the fortunes and futures she needs. She carries a lucky rabbit's foot dyed a deep blue that is almost black. It works so well she buys a pregnant doe from the farmer down Atkins Road. When that rabbit is kindling Carol sit beside the cage and counts to nine. Nine plus the mother was ten, times four is forty times the luck. There is not a single bit of blight on her tomatoes this summer, so that is proof enough. The rabbits eat all the four-leaf clovers in the yard. The math is getting out of hand. Mrs. Brennan and her dog, Fred, herd three escaped sheep up the dirt lane one acre to the north. Carol hurries over to meet them. The roast chicken for dinner is filled with lemon slices and garlic cloves. She ties the wishbone to her collection before going to bed and sleeping facing south.

Let's Recollect the Madness

You are the spawn of

raging river and wild moon

and when I speak of you

my throat clenches like a fist

wrestles the air from my heart.

My sweet mind

sails west in a raft of dreams

setting foot on the shore of the Frisco Bay

laying down and bowing to the great September sky,

smelling Trieste coffee

tasting the olive flavored nights of Columbus Avenue

my memories are slayed

by the blade of your negativity

and the world you created from

the cave of your smoke shrouded mind.

How the juice of the grape

wept rivers upon my tongue

and the wings of the Hummingbird

tap danced the music of life,

while you with the fist of a native warrior

stood naked in Napa valley and

cast poisoned arrows at the Sun.

Where was the rain,

the broken limbs,

the trips to the desert

the battles beneath the Golden Bridge,

you hid in a mist of pills and smoke

meandering along the blues alleys of the Tenderloin

creating your own jigsaw puzzle.

The beating heart of that city,

the dancing vibe of its shoes,

soaked the wings of the dove

that perched on the edge of my soul.

The flower of Haight Ashbury,

the colors of Castro

the tonic breath of the evening fog

reminds river and moon

your memories stew in the cooking pot

and together shall spit forth

a recollection of the madness.

Customer Service

The man had come in to get a haircut because he saw a sign in the window that said "We'll cut your hair anyway you want." He smiled at the barber as he took a seat. As the barber dusted the man's neck with baby powder he asked the man what his name was. He said, "Hey man, what's your name?"

They made eye contact in the giant mirror as the barber wrapped a strip of paper around the man's neck. The man said he had recently changed his name to Klimax, with a 'K,' which he emphasized, and then added that he had chosen that name because it "sounded futuristic."

The barber said, "It's always good to plan ahead." Then he asked the man what kind of haircut he wanted. He said, "Hey man, so what do you want to do with your hair?"

They stared at each other in the mirror again. Then the man used his hands, motioning with both of them and pointing at different parts of his head saying he needed a new start, while explaining that he wanted "the craziest haircut ever."

The barber said, "Then I better get more scissors." The barber opened a drawer and added three more pairs of scissors to the fingers of each hand, six total, then opening and closing them all in a few quick chops, to demonstrate his expert control of the many scissors, he asked the man if six pairs of scissors were enough to make his hair as crazy as the man wanted it to be. He said, "Hey man, do you think these are enough scissors to make your hair crazy like you want? I have boxes of scissors in the back I could go get."

They stared at each other in the mirror, the barber poised to cut, waiting only for Klimax. The man said that six pairs were more than enough, but to really ensure the craziness of his haircut, he asked if the barber could please "wear a blindfold."

The barber said, "You're taking me back to my roots man." Then the barber went on to explain, as he searched for a suitable item to blindfold himself with, that as an amateur barber his old trainer often blindfolded him as a training technique. He said, "I used to cut anything with hair back then, and I could do it blindfolded too. Goats were good practice. Big-headed children were good too because they don't sit still. My trainer had me do it all the time; he said it was the best training a young barber could engage in."

The man looked at him in the mirror with a look of concern and explained that because of his former training he was concerned that the barber wouldn't be able to make his hair crazy enough, that he might, in fact, be too good blindfolded, so he reluctantly asked if the barber wouldn't mind blinding himself instead, because trying to cut hair like that would "really make it crazy."

The barber said conscientiously, "In that state, I might accidentally cut you with the scissors" but the man assured him he wasn't worried about it. Then they looked at each other in the mirror, and looking one last time at the sign in the window, with a very casual shrug, the barber used all six pairs of scissors to blind himself, plunging them into his eyes, and gave Klimax the craziest haircut he's ever had.

Fall's Carriage

Compliant buttons wince around

bundles of escape

Our death trip mostly,

upcountry

recollecting a vague name,

some shady birthrights

of lesser grief.

Devouring the arias of departure's thunderstorm,

begging

the elusions to disenthrall into

hurrahs and dedications

for the wayfarer.

Lingering a bit...

in some upper wilds

weather medium's trembling.

This volatile and cradling day

    takes the continent

                and the kitchen gasps.

A Getaway

The voices were scared and concerned and a little too loud. They were annoying. They floated through the walls and took Tommy out of his show. It was SpongeBob, and yes, he'd seen this episode a few times—maybe twenty, twenty-five, he didn't really keep track—but he still liked to be able to hear what was being said. And his family, always a particularly rude and annoying group of people, did not give his needs much thought. They talked amongst themselves, and Tommy turned the volume up a little bit, and so his family talked a little louder, and so he turned his volume up a little more, and then his family talked even louder—consciously, this time, aware of the skirmish of sounds between the neighboring rooms. SpongeBob began to laugh, and Tommy put the volume to its maximum level, letting the irritating, repetitive laugh make his point for him. It was then that his father came in and shut off the T.V.

Tommy inhaled, getting ready to yell his disapproval, but his dad got the words out first. So Tommy just put on a disgusted, contorted face with hunched shoulders and hands turned up toward the ceiling while his intolerable father explained the gravity of the situation.

Something important. Involves all of us. Time to grow up. Incoming disaster. Need to be together, as a family. Yeah, yeah, yeah, whatever. He got the gist.

His father led him into the room where his mother and older sister sat. His mother had her head in her hands, slowly turning it back and forth. His sister was talking to her, asking what they were all gonna do. His mother wasn't answering, and Tommy didn't like that. No one likes seeing a parent like that. Unsure.

They kept talking. Mostly about how everything was going to be okay, even though Tommy knew it wasn't. Tommy had seen the news, and his family had been watching with him. Something had been…off. But when Tommy pointed out that the news room looked different than usual, and that the local news people were way too calm, his family told him to stop making stuff up and to quit looking for clues that weren't there. Tommy wasn't that upset about it though, because he figured that even if they'd listened, even if they had tried to get somewhere really far away, like Timbuktu or Singapore or Antarctica or something, they still probably wouldn't have made it. They'd only found out yesterday, so even if they'd listened to Tommy's concerns when he first brought them up. No hope.

Tommy said this last part out loud. No hope. He tried to make it sound like it wasn't on purpose, that it was just a quiet, distant, uncontrollable murmur, that he was just naturally smart and genius-like. This, expectedly, drew outrage from his father and sister. His mother didn't respond. His dad and sister yelled at him, and then argued at him, and then explained at him how there was plenty of hope, g-ddamnit, and there's no use in talking like that. Tommy stopped listening, though. He was trying to think where the episode of SpongeBob was right now, commercial breaks included. He guessed somewhere around Plankton and SpongeBob singing the F.U.N. song.

Tommy stayed silent for the rest of the conversation. He stared out the window in between where his sister and mother sat, daydreaming of his T.V. show. Every once in a while, his father would ask for his acknowledgment, which he would give with a simple nod of his head or shrug of his shoulders. Then he would lose himself in the fantasy that would be fulfilled if he could just get back to the T.V. room. Any second now, he thought. There was probably still a good five minutes left, and if he didn't make it, there was a marathon running, anyway. So he could always catch the next episode.

Tommy's dad always told him that, at 10 years old, he was too young to swear. But Tommy knew bullshit when he saw it, and when his dad stood up, clapped his hands, and told everyone to get their stuff together, he couldn't think of the age-appropriate adjective. This time, though, he kept his thoughts to himself.

They all went upstairs, silent and slow and hesitant. His father and mother went to their room, and Tommy peeked in their door to watch them pull out big suitcases and pack them full of clothes and memorabilia. Tommy noticed that his parents left a good half of each suitcase empty. For food, he guessed.

He peered into his sister's room. She was crying, and packing too. But she didn't really know what to bring. She packed clothes, because that was the most obvious choice. She also threw in some pictures, of friends and family and memories that didn't really mean much. Just in case she was the last one and needed some company, he figured. Tommy smiled and felt a little too real when he watched her put his picture in the suitcase, and besides, the next episode of SpongeBob was probably ten minutes in already. He turned away, and went to his room.

Tommy wasn't going to pack. He just wanted to say goodbye. He always liked his room, and he grabbed a suitcase that would stay empty while he admired it all one last time. His eyes passed over his messy desk and his sports posters and his stuffed fox that he hid whenever his friends came up there. Then he looked at the clock on the wall; the second episode of the marathon was just about over. He could always catch the third.

Voices rushed through the house. Loud voices. Not angry, really, just fear masked with anger. Tommy's parents were yelling, and it echoed loudly like everything does in their house, and his sister was yelling and crying even louder than his parents, and—and it was all very loud. Tommy went downstairs and turned on the T.V., the volume all the way up, and now he could barely hear anything besides the obnoxious, high-pitched happy laugh.

Eventually, his father came down, as Tommy suspected he would, and turned off the T.V. Tommy argued a little, just asked for ten more minutes or—or just until the next commercial! His dad said he didn't have time, but Tommy knew it was all he really had time for. He liked the sound of this thought, this clever—well, Tommy didn't know the term for it, but he wanted to say it out loud and be impressive and depressing and real. Instead, he complied, but only because his father dragged him by his shirt to the front door.

No one knew where they were going. Whenever Tommy's sister asked, the answer would just be "South". Tommy knew it wouldn't make a difference. But he didn't feel like getting yelled at again, so when they were all in the living room, gathered by the front door with suitcases in hand, he just nodded like a good boy and went with them. They filled up the trunk of the minivan, and then Tommy remembered his iPod inside, loaded with all his favorite T.V. shows. Against his sister's protests, he ran back inside and up to his room, and rummaged through his various drawers. He found the iPod on his bed, next to his fox, and Tommy didn't like the way his fox was staring at him, so he gave in and decided to take the stuffed animal back to the car. He ran downstairs, his soft fox in one hand, and his iPod in the other, protected in its nice, clear, waterproof case.

They sped off. Tommy plugged his iPod into a charger that was in turn plugged into the cigarette lighter in the back, but he didn't tell his parents he was doing it. He knew they would have a fit about him fiddling with the cigarette lighter because—well, he didn't really know why. They were just very protective, he decided. They were also distracted. His dad was driving the car at an alarming speed. Tommy wasn't sure how fast, exactly, but it was enough that his mother was frantically yelling and pointing and informing his dad that it was a fucking minivan and it can't handle going this fast. His dad said we can't handle going any slower, and Tommy rolled his eyes at the stupidity of his dad's comment. He accepted a worried glance from his sister before plugging in his headphones and enjoying the calm, happy underwater world of Bikini Bottom. It looked nice down there.

Tommy's mother offered him a snack, but he barely noticed and waved it away. They had been driving for quite a while now—four and a half episodes. Tommy almost took his eyes off the iPod to check on his fox or glance out the window and see how far they had gotten, where they were, what kind of environment, what all the other people were doing—but then he decided he really just didn't care.

He got through the whole SpongeBob movie, and half an episode more, before it finally came.

Tommy's sister shrieked, loud enough to overpower the shrieking laugh of SpongeBob. He didn't look, but he could guess what she was screaming about. He could feel all the commotion now; the quick, frantic hand that was shaking his leg, the barely-audible clicks of seat belts and clunks of door locks, the slams of those unlocked doors opening and closing. Then, for a second, it was silent and peaceful, and he enjoyed being alone with his iPod. But soon he heard powerful bangs on his window, and he just shook his head, and the bangs got louder, and he shook his head faster, until finally he looked up, and his family was yelling at him to get out of there, but his door was locked and he wouldn't open it. His dad opened the front door and tried to come around the front seat into the back, and he screamed and swore and pointed out the opposite window, and Tommy looked and saw the giant, behemoth wall of water that he had known would eventually come rushing toward them as it roared on the horizon. His dad pulled and his sister screamed and his mother cried, and Tommy smiled and said just go and batted his dads hands away and wouldn't unbuckle, and his family was screaming even louder and his dad fumbled in the back seat with him and finally his dad got the seat unbuckled but Tommy squirmed out of his father's embrace, and his mother and sister entered the car to try and help, slamming the door behind them, but it was too compact and crowded and their limbs were tangled and it was an awkward endeavor and his sister wasn't strong enough and she was really just taking up space and hindering the urgent task and—and it was all really distracting. Tommy hadn't heard a thing Patrick had said.

It took a good quarter of an episode for the water to reach the minivan. It smashed the car, and engulfed it, and the car tossed and turned in the fray of the flood. Tommy had managed to buckle himself back in, so he wasn't thrown around the car's interior like the rest of his family. Tommy laughed with SpongeBob, as he and Mr. Krabs foiled Plankton's plots yet again. That silly Plankton. He'll never get a Krabby Patty.

The water began to seep into the car. It poured in much more quickly than Tommy thought it would. His father screamed at him, and his sister asked his mom if everything would be okay and his mom pretended not to hear the question. After questioning Tommy's sanity, his father told them all to hyperventilate, because he had heard that it helps you hold your breath longer, and Tommy had heard this too but decided against it. Tommy turned his iPod volume up a little louder, and now his sister's whimpers and his father's encouraging words and his mother's silence were no longer audible. He watched his family huff and puff to the sound of buzzing jellyfish, and then they took one last, over-dramatized giant gulp of air into their lungs. Tommy only let a normal breath enter his own.

It was cold and dirty. The water had finally filled up the minivan, which itself was flipping through the oblivion, and his headphones shorted out. He could no longer ignore the sounds of reality. And sound sounds interesting underwater, Tommy thought, as he listened to the gurgles of his sister and the thunking of a door handle that wouldn't open. They had odd, thick echoes to them. Luckily, though, the iPod still played, locked safely away in its waterproof case. Tommy couldn't hear what SpongeBob was saying to Sandy, outfitted in Karate gear and flipping through the sea, but he had seen this episode enough times to know the gist. That was good enough.

Tommy's father and mother gave up trying to open the door. They couldn't manage to break the windows, either. Tommy's mother held his sister, and he couldn't see their tears but he saw her head bobbing up and down in convulsive jumps. His sister's face was buried in his mother's chest, and his father joined in. Tommy's eyes flicked from the screen to his family, back and forth, barely noticing the difference between the cartoon bubbles and the real ones, sporadic as they were, and he went over to join them. With one arm, he embraced the huddle, and with the other, he held his iPod, reaching around the huddle and holding it in back of his family where they wouldn't see it even if they opened their eyes. He watched it play between his sister's and mother's foreheads, now pressed against each other. His dad's head was tilted towards what might have been the sky.

Eventually, that urge to breathe became overpowering. Tommy's fox floated through the car, along with long-lost toys from happy meals and bouncy balls and some empty candy wrappers that escaped from under the seats and further polluted the already dirty water that was all around him. Tommy kept his cold, stinging eyes glued to the screen as inevitability inevitably took its course.

Drowning was not a pleasant experience. Tommy thought, based on all the movies and T.V. shows he'd seen, that it would happen, it would suck, and then it would be over. But this felt like it was going on for a long time. It was painful. And cold, too. He was wondering why he hadn't passed out or died yet, but maybe it had really only been a minute or so and it just felt like longer. The water crept up around his nostrils, and he resisted, hoping he would just pass out already, and he watched SpongeBob watch a sunset with Squidward while frigid liquid seeped into his ears and clawed into his sinuses. He fought the urge to breathe as best he could, willing himself to become unconscious and forcing his squinting eyes to focus on the iPod, but his instincts took over and Tommy finally let go, snorting and gulping mouth-and-nose-fulls of water into his lungs. He felt arms squeeze him tighter as he tried to scream and cry with the last bit of breath in the deepest pits of his lungs, and then his head felt flushed and his vision blurred and his chest lurched, and he slipped into a dark peace, instincts telling him that it was finally ending.

But that's not how drowning works. A minute later, his body forced itself awake, and in a tormented haze his body tried one last time to vomit the water in his lungs and take in new air, but there was no air to take, only cold, dirty water, and in this last second of his life, in agony and bliss, Tommy choked and gagged and drowned, sucking and spewing regurgitated water. He was no longer aware of where he was or why he was there, and while his body shook, unable to control itself, his eyes focused on the strange, glowing screen between two quivering masses, and as Tommy's eyes began to shut, they processed SpongeBob laughing and he could practically hear that annoying, happy, gleeful, high-pitched giggle through the rushing in his ears and the pain in his lungs and the screaming in his head.

And somewhere, way in the back of his oxygen-deprived brain, a signal was released that told him everything was normal, that everything would probably be okay.

The Stage in Question

It's the stage where you take

your time through the junk mail

for what each item has to say,

       where you keep

finding yourself buying

the expressions of care.

Bracketing 'Outside' Problems

We only think about "inside" problems,

problems within the known universe:

pandemics, wars, asteroids, the sun using up its fuel.

But there's always that analogue

to child hands clapping a bubble.

Breaking the Bread

My vision kept switching between clarity and haze. I could feel redness in my eyes and the waves of last night's liquor sloshing in my stomach.

Through the back window of my grandmother's cottage, I saw my brothers arranging lawn chairs into a perfect circle beneath the grapefruit tree. My older brother James, who'd already broken the bread two years back, wore a sapphire shirt and his best Sunday pants. He looked handsome. Riley, just 14, looked tiny in his clothes, probably Christmas presents from my aunt or uncle.

Behind me, I could hear my mother and the other sisters scurrying through the kitchen and den like field mice. One of the children could not tie his shoes. An old woman needed help using the restroom. The bustle made my head sweat cheap tequila.

I shifted my weight to my heels. I hadn't worn my buckle-strap Church shoes since the week before I left for school. My mother had to dig them out of my closet, dust them off and shine them. She asked me how I could have left them behind. I pretended not to hear her.

My dress made me uncomfortable. It hung loose off my shoulders, dark and plain gray, with a white belt and frilly lace that tickled my ankles. The belt pressed the fabric against my skin at the waist. I wondered if anyone could tell I was wearing a thong. Bright pink.

A few of the eldest men walked outside carrying a small table with a covered, woven basket on top. They all wore black from head to toe, neatly tucked and finely-pressed shirts, looking like Johnny Cash if he'd straightened up and found Jesus.

One of the men, whose name I often forgot, danced a second when a ripe grapefruit fell from the tree to his feet. Maybe he did have a little Cash in him.

My grandfather, the leader of The Meeting, came up behind me and placed his arm on my shoulder. I turned to look up at him and noticed his eyebrows first as I always did. They stretched forward and out and curled up; got a little bit of the devil inside of him, my grandmother would say.

"This is a blessed day, my dear," he said through a wide smile. "Great strength comes when one accepts His Spirit into one's body."

"Yes, grandfather."

He began to walk out towards the yard and I followed him, quickly tying my veil around my head. I sat down silently beside my mother who brushed at my leg, straightening a wrinkle. She smiled briefly; perhaps it was a wince.

All eyes turned toward my grandfather who looked like a giant among the seated crowd.

"Thank you, oh Lord, for bringing Your children before us today."

Everyone bowed their heads, but I tilted my neck back when I saw a massive grapefruit dangling from a branch above my mother's father.

"To accept You as their Savior, their Shepherd in this life and the next."

There were dozens of them, spread throughout the tree, some in clusters, some alone, all golden and glistening in the rising Minnesota sun. The tree branches hung like a willow under the weight of the orbs. I glanced over at Mr. Cash.

They went down, down, down, and the flames went higher.

"My own granddaughter is here to allow You to guide her, oh wise God."

My grandfather motioned to me and I quickly dropped my head.

"We pray You guide her and all Your children with Your love, Amen."

The congregation echoed in unison; I forgot again to say it with them and my mother gave me a nudge.

My mother was a feeble woman, born with a fearful heart and sad eyes. Her lids drooped towards the outside of her sunken cheekbones, and made her always appear on the verge of tears. I could tell she was worried. Not just about me, but my soul. When I told her I wanted to go to school in California, she laughed for a second and then cried for a week. It was as if I had slapped her across the face. She held her cheek and kept repeating words I hated like, "fornicators" and "sanctity." They poured from her lips until the day I finally left.

She still believed that I was breaking bread by my own recognizance, that it really was the gospel, not the Sex Pistols, that I listened to on my headphones.

She smiled big now, and it made me suddenly feel guilty about my choice of underwear.

Several men rose, their heads surrounded by grapefruit halos, and spoke briefly about God's love and their children and the joy of the day and the glory and the grace and the Rise and the Fall. The women were silent.

After Mr. Cash read a verse, it was time for the ceremony to begin. There were four of us that day who were breaking for the first time. My grandfather stood and lifted the cover off the basket of bread. He poured red wine with a torn label into four small Dixie cups with blue dinosaurs on them. A snort got stuck in the back of my throat.

I recognized the cups from my grandmother's bathroom. She would fill them with mouthwash for each of us kids on nights when we would stay with her. We'd swirl the minty liquid in our mouths then spit it out, clearing out all the bacteria.

That day we were not supposed to spit. That day it was not mouthwash. It was the blood of Christ, or Two Buck Chuck really, and it would clear away our sins. The thought of more alcohol made me sway. It hadn't been two hours since I'd sworn off the stuff completely, like I'd done so many times before.

The "new" children were told to form a line in front of the table. I stood behind a girl named Maddie, who used to play house with me when we were younger. She was in her first year at seminary school, the pride of The Meeting. I stared and wondered what kind of panties she wore. Something told me they were white, pure.

Maddie stood behind two tall boys I didn't know. I looked up at the cowlicks struggling to break free on the backs of their hairsprayed heads.

My grandfather began the ceremony.

My eyes wandered up again towards a small cluster of grapefruit. They looked so heavy. If Newton had been hit on the head with one of those babies, he might not have lived to tell his theory. Gravity seemed to be doing all it could to draw the fruits down to the ground, but after all, there was little belief of science in this group, so they hung tight.

Grandfather's voice was passionate and deep, but I paid no attention. I started to envision a sudden, terrifying shower of ripened fruit. My mind filled with the thought of them falling from the trees like tart hand grenades.

The first boy knelt, drank the wine, and ate the bread.

I imagined the pink, pulpy shrapnel exploding on contact, spewing all over the congregation's spotless attire. I could see the juice squirting into the eyes of all the ones hell-bent on heaven.

The second boy knelt, drank the wine, and ate the bread.

For the ones lucky enough to avoid the spray, I imagined them being clunked on the head by the massive spheres crashing down like meteorites. It would be Revelations, but with more pastel colors, a golden apocalypse.

Maddie knelt, drank the wine, and ate the bread.

My mother looked at me, her white teeth clenched tightly in a nervous smile. My grandfather grinned from ear to ear, reached forward, and offered a crumb of crust and a cup stained red.

I thought I could feel the ground shaking from all the falling grapefruit. I wished for the pandemonium. I prayed for knockouts from fists of fruit. As my grandfather offered me Jesus in a Dixie cup, I couldn't help but imagine the downfall of every last one of us. What a sweet, sweet escape it would have been.

And the Paintings Blew Wildly All Over the Dark Street

** title from Roxana Robinson's *Georgia O'Keeffe*, p.220

in the midst of the work
the moment is inviolate

the shapes emerge as if
    from hiding
the colors bleed without
    consent
collect like a gathering storm
    and the result is a surprise but not
    really

a marriage of free will and
serendipity
where one ends and the other begins is a
mystery

unlike him she doesn't allow visitors
works only alone
works in progress are never shown and failures
are destroyed

the clarity of water
the eternity of bones
the perfection of nature begging
to be reinvented

Love Like Light

They were gone for a while – out by the lake, watching children chase each other across the grass and around the crowds of geese who pressed against couples on blankets until flustered young men tossed half-eaten sandwiches their way. Sarah stood apart, laughing, slapping her hands against her thighs through the thin material of a pale blue cotton dress spangled with jasmine. Her laugh was a booming thing, which people thought was strange because she was so small – maybe no more than five feet and three inches, weighing about a hundred pounds. Ethan, who was tall with thick, tan limbs, wrapped his arms around her sun-warmed shoulders and kissed her. His dark head pressed next to her blond one, both crowned with a ring of light from the sun.

If you ask people, they would say the grass was green that day. A vivid sort of green in the afternoon sun—a color you don't forget. The ducks preened themselves in the shade stretching over the muddy banks where the clear water was murky. A brown mallard waddled through the bright grass near the ankles of two lovers who held each other recklessly.

When Sarah and Ethan walked into the house, kissing firmly as the door closed, they only had eyes for each other. Maybe that's what really made John do it. Sarah was a woman made of light. And when the couple walked through the door Sarah's light was shining for Ethan – unmistakably, unapologetically.

Ethan was not expecting John to be there waiting. "A man has pride," he'd said to us over dinner at a small tapas restaurant with poor lighting and ironically large portions, "a man knows when to move on." His lack of concern seemed reasonable. Months had passed, locks changed once and then again when the cat went missing, a new kitten adopted, boxes moved in to replace the boxes moved out.

Sarah was surprised to see John and maybe even a little relieved. "I've been expecting you," she said.

She was always so cool. She might have smoothed her dress and offered him a drink, then poured two fingers of scotch and handed it over in her imperious manner – California's answer to Katherine Hepburn, a woman who could also spread her thin-bodied presence through a room. But John had already disengaged the safety. He had waited there all afternoon, considering his purpose; wiping sweaty palms over his buttoned denim shirt with the loose tail that always seemed to come un-tucked even when he held still.

Sarah took four shots; one to the face – her strong-boned, open face – then bled a mess onto the carpet. Ethan was hit in the chest, the bullet nicked his lung and he drowned in his own blood, which then spilled out onto the carpet and spread towards Sarah's puddle. They left deep stains in a wheat-colored carpet that couldn't be lifted.

John only needed the one bullet, though he had brought extra – left them stacked neatly on the kitchen table surrounded by the smell of ashes – the pictures and the his and hers bathroom towels he set on fire and dropped in the kitchen sink to burn while he waited. The kitchen will be aired out then repainted, but people will always wonder if someone was careless and left the oven running.

The relator will also have hardwood floors installed before selling the house to a young couple. The wife will take coats and usher her friends across that floor. The husband will clap shoulders, spill drinks, and make bad jokes about lawyers over that floor. Their first baby will play there, then the second and third. And when the kids are at his mother's house, they will make love there. She'll cry loudly in his ears. They will come together, naked on that floor. The house is only a box for the small lives it contains. Seasons change. Light moves through the windows. The walls are repainted. The floors are redone.

The newspaper didn't say where Sarah, Ethan, and John were in the house or how they looked when they were found. The article was a collage of useless words: history of violence, homicide, suicide. The sum of a lifetime of being loved and loving others can be found in three columns of black letters, and then the most important things get left out. But I know Sarah would have reached for Ethan – she would have died with her hand in his.

I put the paper down and wait for Peter to come home. The funeral is tomorrow. We will sit in a sea of stiff and dark people. We will wait for the service to end before hugging her parents who will be as thin and drawn as they have ever been in their lives. And I will wait on the church steps while Peter brings the car around. I will feel the warmth of the sun on my shoulders. Children will run around the sidewalks, chasing each other and picking daisies from planter boxes; their parents too tired to scold. Sour cherries will swell on the branches of the trees that line the sidewalk. The sun will be in the middle of the sky. A vivid, blue burning sky. It will be the early afternoon – everything will be bright.

Iberian

Come and see these Iberian women with their two hearts. They grow like twin mum flowers, their feet are lightly raised, their steps soft and permanent. These dark haired impossible women, twisting their necks like burnt canaries. In Badajoz they march through the streets in hundreds, as if they do not even exist.

Yemen

The succulent elbow of Yemen is somehow mispronouncing my name. My gourd shaped name, which is made from snow and the breath of all-white cows. She has raised syllables from lightning-shaped sand, and thrown her voice with dead misplaced gulls.

AUTHORS

Rachel Adams

Rachel Adams is a Baltimore native and longtime resident of Washington, DC, the editor of several publications at a nonprofit advocacy association, the founder and editor of *Lines + Stars*, and a freelance writer. Her poetry has previously been published in *Blueline, Arsenic Lobster, Town Creek Poetry, Four and Twenty, Ophelia Street, Grasslimb, Urbanite Baltimore, Melusine, Memoir,* and *The Conium Review* and is forthcoming in *Free State Review* and *The North American Review.* She received her BA in English from the Catholic University of America and her MA in writing from the Johns Hopkins University.

Alan Britt

Alan Britt's interview with the Library of Congress for *The Poet and the Poem* is up at will air on Pacifica Radio in January 2013. His interview with *Minnesota Review* is up at minnesotareview.wordpress.com. He read poems at the World Trade Center/Tribute WTC Visitor Center in Manhattan/NYC, April 2012, at the We Are You Project, Wilmer Jennings Gallery, East Village/NYC, April 2012, and at New Jersey City University's *Ten Year 9/11 Commemoration* in Jersey City, NJ, September 2011. His poem, "September 11, 2001," appeared in *International Gallerie: Poetry in Art/Art in Poetry Issue,* v13 No.2 (India): 2011. His recent book is "Alone with the Terrible Universe" (*CypressBooks* 2011). Recent anthologies include "Emergency Verse: Poetry in Defence of the Welfare State," by *Caparison* an imprint of *The Recusant,* United Kingdom: 2011; "The Poet's Cookbook: 33 American Poets with German Translations," *Forest Woods Media Productions/Goerthe Institute,* Washington, DC: 2010; "American Poets Against the War," *Metropolitan Arts Press,* Chicago/Athens/Dublin: 2009 and "Vapor transatlántico (Transatlantic Steamer)," bi-lingual anthology of Latin American and North American poets, *Hofstra University Press/Fondo de Cultura Económica de Mexico/Universidad Nacional Mayor de San Marcos de Peru,* 2008. Alan currently teaches English/Creative Writing at Towson University and lives in Reisterstown, Maryland with his wife, daughter, two Bouviers des Flandres, one Bichon Frise and two formally feral cats. He is the Book Review Editor for *Ragazine.*

Betsy Brown

Betsy Brown's book "Year of Morphines" (*LSU Press*) was a *National Poetry Series* winner. Her poems have appeared in recent issues of *Antioch Review, B O D Y, Conduit, Conte, H_NGM_N,* and *Prairie Schooner.*

Stephen Byrne

Stephen Byrne is a chef from Galway west Ireland. His work has been published in various places in Ireland and recently in *Emerge Literary Journal, The Dead Beats, The Rusty Nail, Writing.com Anthology, The Big Issue* and *The Galway Review.* His first book, a collaboration of poets called "Wayword Tuesdays" was published in November. He was a featured reader at the *Over the Edge* readings Galway and was shortlisted for last year's *Over the Edge* poetry competition.

Lisa J. Cihlar

Lisa J. Cihlar's poems appeared in *The South Dakota Review, Green Mountains Review, Crab Creek Review, Blackbird,* and *The Prose-Poem Project.* One of her poems was nominated for a Pushcart Prize. Her chapbook, "The Insomniac's House," is available from *Dancing Girl Press* and a second chapbook, "This is How She Fails," is available from *Crisis Chronicles Press.* She lives in rural southern Wisconsin.

Karen Cook

Karen Cook has been writing short stories and poetry since childhood. Her first published piece, an essay "on being a girl," was published in a college sociology textbook. She writes it all: short stories, articles, poetry, essays, and -- most recently -- a novel set in France, in the 14th century. She has had four short stories, a poem, and over 50 articles published. After writing, and her family, Karen's great love is traveling. "I find inspiration wherever I go," she says. "My novel is based on a visit to a prehistoric site in Brittany that I visited in 2009. The standing stones I saw there became a character in my story."

Alissa M. Fehlbaum

Alissa M. Fehlbaum is working on her MFA at the University of Colorado at Boulder, where she also teaches creative writing. She was raised in Mabank, Texas, and received her BA from the University of North Texas. Her work has been featured in *Collective Fallout, Postcard Shorts* and *Thunderdome Magazine.*

Maureen Foster

Maureen Foster is the author of three novels; "Beginners," "Sparks," and "Home Front." Her essays, poetry, and short fiction have appeared in *The Los Angeles Times, The Pacific Review, Word River, Burning Word,* and many other publications. Maureen grew up in New York and presently lives in Santa Cruz, where she teaches film and composition at the University of California.

Troy Frings

Troy lives in northern New Jersey where he attends graduate school. A coffee aficionado, he is still waiting for that one storied caffeine boost to get him through his first novel.

Michael V. Gibson

Michael V. Gibson is an editor, language teacher and tutor, itinerant writer, and perpetually impermanent lodger. His work has previously appeared in the journals *Panâche* and *Cardinal Sins*, where he won the category prize for short fiction. He currently divides his time between Asia and North America.

Andrew Hamilton

Andrew Hamilton graduated from the University of Tennessee in May of 2012 where he won the school's coveted Margaret Artley Woodruff award, Bain-Swiggett traditional poetry prize, and Knickerbocker non-traditional poetry prize. His short story "Surface Tension" was recently announced runner-up for the *Saturday Evening Post*'s Great American Fiction Competition. He is now applying to graduate schools to achieve his MFA. Along with the *Post,* his work has been accepted for publication by *BlazeVOX, Yes, Poetry, Emerge Literary Journal, P.Q. Leer,* and *Glassworks*.

Shannon Hanks-Mackey

Shannon Hanks-Mackey studies Comparative Literature and Cinema Studies at the University of Washington. A few of the myriad interests that hold her attention are plant medicine, mycology and folklore. She is also working towards becoming a funeral director & death midwife. Her work has been published in *Hoarse & Alice Blue* and will appear in an upcoming edition of *The Black Scholar*. Mostly. she's a bibliomaniac who likes to laugh and crack-wise until someone gets hurt.

Tayler Heusten
Tayler Heuston, California-native, lives in Santa Barbara where she spends much of her spare time reading "The Habit of Being" and falling in love with Flannery O'Connor. Her fiction has been published by *RiverLit*.

Kamden Hilliard
Kamden Hilliard is a student at Sarah Lawrence College and a 2012 Davidson Laureate in Literature. He has been published (or has forthcoming work) in *Emerge Literary Journal*, *Bellow Literary Journal*, *The Orange Room Review*, and other places. If Kamden wasn't writing, he'd be very sad - or a scientist.

René Houtrides
René Houtrides's short stories have appeared in *The Georgia Review*, *New Ohio Review*, *The Mississippi Review*, and a special fiction supplement of *The Woodstock Times*. One of her *Georgia Review* stories was included in that journal's Spring 2011 issue, given over to a retrospective of its finest short stories from the past 25 years. She was a staff writer for *The Woodstock Times* for five years, during which time she received a New York Press Association Award (first place) for best sports/outdoor column. More than half a dozen of her essays have aired on WAMC Public Radio. One of her plays, *Calamity Jane*, was produced in New York City; and a great deal of her original theater material was performed at theaters throughout the United States and on national television. She received an MFA in creative writing from Bard College and is currently on the faculty of Juilliard's drama division. She was born and raised near Manhattan's Little Italy and Chinatown.

M.A. Istvan Jr.
M.A. Istvan Jr. is pursuing a PhD in Philosophy and an MA in English at Texas A&M. His poetry has appeared in the *Moose & Pussy* and will next appear in the *Penwood Review*.

Rich Ives
Rich Ives is the 2009 winner of the Francis Locke Memorial Poetry Award from *Bitter Oleander* and the 2012 winner of the Creative Nonfiction Prize from *Thin Air* magazine. The Spring 2011 *Bitter*

Oleander contains a feature including an interview and 18 of his hybrid works.

Brian Kayser
Brian Kayser is a writer who lives in Charlottesville, Virginia. Brian's fiction has appeared in *34th Parallel Magazine, Alliterati Magazine, Bursting Plethora, Down Dirty Word, Eunoia Review, Misfits Miscellany, Open Window Review, The Orris Journal, Shadows Express, The Toucan Online, The Write Room,* and *Writing Raw.* He was been editor-in-chief at HipHopGame.com from 2003-2012, where he interviewed and written about a variety of hip-hop artists. Brian's writings about music have also appeared in *The Source* and various websites and magazines.

Dan Kennard
Dan Kennard earned his MFA from Florida Atlantic University in May 2011 and now resides in Fort Pierce, FL where he is a Composition and Literature instructor at Keiser University. He also maintains a monthly fiction blog at litcoms.com where he writes a literature-sitcom called "Virgil Inhibited."

Dave Kostos
Dave Kostos is a writer from Salem, Massachusetts currently finishing his Bachelor degree studies in English and Psychology. This is his first published work, though hopefully far from his last.

Nate Musser
Nate Musser is currently a student writing out of Long Beach. His works have been published in *The Legendary* and with *Bank-Heavy Press.* At the moment, his purpose in life is to find his purpose in life.

Phillip Neilsen
Philip Neilsen is a poet and fiction writer based in Australia where he teaches writing at Queensland University of Technology. His most recent books are "Without an Alibi" (his fifth poetry collection) and "The Cambridge Companion to Creative Writing" (co-edited with David Morley).

Heather E. Pecoraro
Heather Elise Pecoraro lives in Nebraska with her best friends and lop-eared rabbit, Haku. When she is not nestled away somewhere with her

nose buried in a book, she is writing poems or creating odd acrylic abstractions. Her poetry has been included in *Borderline Poetry*, *Northwind Magazine*, *Petrichor Review*, and *SPILT* magazine. She is greatly inspired and influenced by the works of Hermann Hesse, Kurt Vonnegut, Allen Ginsberg, T.S. Eliot, and E.E. Cummings (to name a few!).

Dianne Post
Dianne Post is an international human rights attorney who works primarily on gender-based violence against women and children. She lives in Arizona with the sun.

Aaron Saylor
Aaron Saylor lives in the Louisville, KY area with his wife, Leslie. He is also the author of "Sewerville: A Southern Gangster Novel," published in November 2012 by *Point Nine Publishing*.

Olivia Somes
Olivia Somes earned a BA in Creative Writing and English Literature in 2012 at California State University, Long Beach where she is currently a graduate student in the MFA program. You can find her poems in *Verdad* and several issues of *Bankheavy Press*. In the summer, *Bankheavy Press* published Olivia's first Chapbook, a joint effort with Karie McNeley, called "Life After Purgatory."

Alex Stuart
Alex Stuart is a Boston native who studies at the University of Michigan. He hopes to become a successful writer and marine biologist, but figures he might as well add "supermodel" and "secret agent" to that list. For now, he frequently writes, studies, and tries to keep compromising photos off of Facebook. Can't have that coming back to bite him when he's a pulitzer-prize-nobel-prize-winning President of the World.

Gergory Zorko
Gregory Zorko is a 22 year old poet and history student. His work has been published in *NANO Fiction*, *Busk*, and *Burning Word Magazine* among others. He lives and works in upstate New York.

Visit www.crackthespine.com to subscribe to our weekly digital magazine or to review our submission guidelines.

www.ingramcontent.com/pod-product-compliance
Lightning Source LLC
Chambersburg PA
CBHW070554180626
46817CB00005B/1836